A LOCKET TO DIE FOR

When we last entered the small hamlet of Blackstone, we were thrust into darkest shadows. Looming high on the hill above town was the old Asylum . . . once scheduled for demolition, but still standing tall. The McGuire family was first to feel the destructive reach of its chilling legacy. For after an "innocent" gift, an antique doll, was anonymously delivered to the McGuires' doorstep, little Megan cradled it to her heart—and, unknowing, brought pure evil into her home.

Now, in the black of night, another strange package has arrived in someone's unsuspecting arms. Inside: a shiny silver locket. Who would ever suspect that a lovely piece of jewelry could wreak such hell and havoc?

THE BLACKSTONE
CHRONICLES
TWIST OF FATE:
THE LOCKET

By John Saul:

SUFFER THE CHILDREN
PUNISH THE SINNERS
CRY FOR THE STRANGERS
COMES THE BLIND FURY
WHEN THE WIND BLOWS
THE GOD PROJECT
NATHANIEL
BRAINCHILD
HELLFIRE
THE UNWANTED
THE UNLOVED
CREATURE
SECOND CHILD
SLEEPWALK
DARKNESS
SHADOWS
GUARDIAN*
THE HOMING*
BLACK LIGHTNING*
THE BLACKSTONE CHRONICLES:
  Part 1—AN EYE FOR AN EYE: THE DOLL*
  Part 2—TWIST OF FATE: THE LOCKET*

*Published by Fawcett Books

THE BLACKSTONE CHRONICLES

PART 2
TWIST OF FATE: THE LOCKET

John Saul

FAWCETT CREST • NEW YORK

A Fawcett Crest Book
Published by Ballantine Books
Copyright © 1997 by John Saul

All rights reserved under International and Pan-American Copyright Conventions. Published in the United States by Ballantine Books, a division of Random House, Inc., New York, and simultaneously in Canada by Random House of Canada Limited, Toronto.

http://www.randomhouse.com

Library of Congress Catalog Card Number: 96-90778

ISBN 0-449-22784-7

Manufactured in the United States of America

First Edition: March 1997

10   9   8   7   6   5   4   3   2   1

*For Linda, with
hugs and kisses*

Prelude

The full moon stood high in the night sky above Blackstone, bathing the stones of the old Asylum atop North Hill in a silvery glow, even penetrating the thick layers of grime that covered its windows so that its dusty rooms were suffused with a dim light. Though the dark figure who moved silently through these rooms needed no light to guide him, the luminescence allowed him to pause now and then to savor the memories this place held for him: vivid memories. Images as sharp and clear as if the events they depicted had occurred only yesterday. He was their keeper, even if those same memories had faded from the minds of the very few in Blackstone who might have shared them.

And this room, with its shelves filled with mementos, was his sanctuary, his museum, to which he had added something new.

It was an ancient ledger, which he'd come upon in one of the basement storerooms. Covered in faded red leather, it was like the ones used in years gone by, in which were recorded all the minutiae of the Asylum's busy life. Taking the book to the shelf-lined, square room, he stroked its cover with all the sensual gentleness with which a man might stroke the skin of a beautiful woman. Hoping it might jog delicious memories even his brilliant mind might have mislaid, he finally opened its cover, only to feel a pang of bitter disappointment: despite its age, its yellowed leaves proved blank. Then disappointment

1

gave way to a tingling excitement. There would be a new use for the book, an important use.

An album!

An album containing accounts of the madness unleashed upon the town that had spurned him.

Now, hunched over the album in the dim moonlight, he opened its cover and read once more the familiar words of the two articles he had painstakingly clipped and carefully pasted to the brittle pages within.

The first described the suicide of Elizabeth Conger McGuire, despondent over the premature birth—and death—of her son.

Nowhere had the newspaper account mentioned the beautiful doll that arrived at the McGuires' a few short days before Elizabeth's death, returning at last to the house from which it had been carried so many years ago in the arms of a child who had entered this very building, never to leave it again.

The second article, lovingly pasted into the album, had appeared three days later, noting the burial of Elizabeth McGuire and listing all the people who had gone to the cemetery to mourn her.

People who, soon enough, would be mourned themselves.

Closing the album, the dark figure caressed its cover once again, shivering with anticipation as he imagined the stories it soon would contain.

Then, as the moon began to drop in the sky and dark shadows edged up the walls, he touched again the object he had decided to deliver next.

The beautiful heart-shaped locket, in which was contained a lock of hair . . .

Prologue

"*Lorena.*"

It wasn't her real name, but it was a name she decided she liked. For today at least, it would be hers.

Perhaps she would use it again tomorrow, but perhaps not.

And no last name. Never a last name.

Not even a made-up one.

Too easy to make a mistake if you used a last name. You could accidentally use your real initials, and give yourself away. Not that Lorena would ever make such a mistake, since she hadn't even risked using a first name that started with her real initial since she'd come here.

They'd told her it was a hospital, but the moment she saw the stone walls, she knew they were lying. It was a prison—and dressing the guards as doctors and nurses hadn't fooled Lorena for a minute. It hadn't fooled the people who were watching her either. They were already there, waiting for her. She'd felt their eyes on her from the moment she came through the huge oak door and heard it slam shut behind her—imprisoning her.

Over the months she'd been here, though, Lorena developed a few tricks of her own. She'd never spoken her real name out loud; trained herself even to keep from thinking it, since some of her enemies had learned to read her mind. She'd learned to make herself inconspicuous, doing nothing that would draw attention to herself, barely moving, never speaking.

3

She spent most of her time simply sitting in the chair. It was an ugly chair, a horrible chair, covered with a hideous green material that felt sticky when she touched it, which she tried not to do: that sticky stuff might be some kind of poison with which her enemies were trying to kill her. She thought about finding another chair to sit in, but that would only let them know she'd caught on to what they were trying to do, and inspire them to try something else.

Lorena sat perfectly still. The slightest movement, even the blink of an eye, could give her away almost as quickly as using her real name. Some of them had been watching her for so long that she was certain they could recognize her by the slightest gesture.

The way she brushed her hair back from her face.

Even the way she tilted her head.

Her enemies were everywhere. And still they came.

Ever watchful, never letting down her guard, today she'd spotted a new one.

This time it was a well-dressed woman—exactly the kind of woman who used to pretend to be her friend back in the days before she'd caught on to the plot. This woman was younger than her, forty, with long dark hair that she had swept into an elaborate French twist at the back of her head. She wore a silk dress in the darkest shade of midnight blue. Lorena immediately recognized its distinctive cut and flair, which could only have come from Monsieur Worth in Paris. Lorena herself had been fitted in his salon when she'd traveled on the Lusitania *to Europe the year before they sank it.*

The woman was talking to the warden, who still pretended he was a doctor even though Lorena had made it perfectly clear to him that she knew exactly who he really was. Every few minutes the woman's eyes flicked in her direction. Each time, Lorena wondered if the woman was truly foolish enough to think she didn't notice.

Another surreptitious glance.

Lorena felt the familiar fear quicken inside her. They were watching her, talking about her. Despite the charade they were playing out—that they had eyes only for each other—they weren't fooling her at all.

They weren't just watching her.

They were plotting against her.

A plot Lorena wouldn't—couldn't—let succeed.

The woman's eyes flicked nervously to the patient who had been sitting in the dayroom, unmoving, from the moment she and the doctor slipped in to steal a few minutes alone together. When the doctor had first suggested to the woman that she volunteer to spend a few hours each week at the Asylum, the idea hadn't appealed to her at all. In fact, though she'd never admitted it to anyone, she'd always been a little afraid of the forbidding building on the top of North Hill. But the more she thought about it, the more convinced she became that her lover was right—as a volunteer, no one would question her reasons for coming up here. Her husband would be none the wiser, and her friends would be completely thrown off the scent.

Today, as she had nearly every day since the affair had begun a month ago, she'd driven up the hill to offer her services. She had talked to some of the patients, read a story to an odd little boy, played cards with a sad-eyed old man. All the time waiting for her lover to appear. Then, there he was, taking her gently by the arm, escorting her through the corridors until finally, a little while ago, they'd come into this room, which was empty save for the woman in the chair.

"She doesn't even know we're here," he assured her, slipping his arms around her and pulling her toward him, his lips nuzzling at her throat. Despite the thrill of *excitement that ran through her body, the woman pulled away from him, her eyes flicking toward the patient in the chair.*

"What's wrong with her?" she asked. "Why doesn't she move?"

"She's delusional." He glanced at the patient. "She thinks if she holds still, her 'enemies' can't see her." Reaching into the pocket of his white coat, he pulled out a small box. "I have something for you." He put the box into her hands. "Something to celebrate our being together."

The woman gazed at the pale blue box, recognizing its origin immediately. Her heart beating a little faster, she undid the white silk ribbon and lifted off the lid. Inside there was a soft velvet pouch; inside the pouch was a tiny locket.

In the shape of a heart, it was covered with silver filigree, and when she pressed on the tiny catch to open it, the woman found a lock of hair pressed under the glass where a picture could have gone.

Taking the locket from the woman's hands, the doctor unhooked its chain and, as she turned around, placed the chain around her neck and fastened it. As she turned back to face him, he leaned down and pressed his lips against her neck.

A flush of heat coursed through her body; the woman closed her eyes.

Lorena watched it all—watched them whisper to each other, watched them glance at her, then watched them whisper again. She watched the woman open the box and take out the locket; watched her open it. As the "doctor" put it around the woman's neck, Lorena suddenly knew what was contained inside the silver heart.

Lies.

The locket was filled with lies about her, lies that the woman would carry out and spread among her enemies.

As the "doctor" bent down once more to whisper into the woman's ear, Lorena leaped from the chair and scuttled across the room, her fingers already extended so that before the woman could turn away, Lorena had already snatched the locket from her neck, the thin silver chain breaking.

She backed away, the locket clutched in her hand, her wary eyes watching to see what they would do.

The "doctor" moved toward her. "Give it to me," he said quietly, holding out his hand.

Lorena backed farther away, her fingers clenched on the tiny locket.

"What's she going to do with it?" she heard the woman ask.

As the "doctor" moved toward her once again, Lorena edged backward until the wall stopped her, then scrabbled crabwise along the wall until she could go no farther. Cornered, she watched the "doctor" move closer to her. Her eyes flicked over the room, searching for some means of escape, but there was none. The "doctor" reached toward her once again, but Lorena, far more clever than he, had already figured out what to do.

Before his hand could close on her wrist, then pry her fingers loose from the tiny piece of jewelry, her own hand went to her mouth.

In an instant, she swallowed the locket.

"You shouldn't have done that," she heard the "doctor" say, but it didn't matter, because now the locket was safely out of his reach.

Lorena, knowing she'd won, began to laugh. Her laughter built, filling the room with a raucous sound that didn't die away until three "orderlies" came in and circled around her. Then Lorena's laughter suddenly became a scream of terror.

* * *

They were in a room in the basement of the Asylum. It was equipped with a metal table. Above the table a bright light was suspended.

The orderlies, having strapped the patient to the table, had disappeared. Now, as the woman gazed at the patient's terrified eyes, she wished she'd never come here today.

Indeed, she wished she'd never met the doctor at all.

"Perhaps you should wait outside," he said.

Making no reply, the woman started out of the room, but before she passed through the doorway, she turned around and glanced back.

A scalpel glimmered in her lover's hand.

Stepping quickly out of the room, the woman pulled the door closed behind her as if the act alone could shut what she'd just seen out of her mind. But the scream she heard a moment later seared the scene into her memory forever.

The first scream was followed by another, and then another, and for just an instant the woman was certain that someone would appear, would burst from the stairs at the end of the corridor to stop whatever was happening behind the closed door.

But no one came. Slowly, the screams died away, to be replaced by a deathly silence.

At last, when she thought she could take it no more, the door opened and the doctor stepped out. Before he pulled the door closed behind him, the woman caught a glimpse of the room beyond.

The patient, her face gray, still lay strapped to the operating table.

Her eyes, open and lifeless, seemed to be staring at the woman.

Blood oozed from her eviscerated belly, and crimson

threads were strung from the edge of the table to the scarlet pool on the floor.

The door closed.

The doctor pressed the locket into the woman's hand, still warm with the heat of the patient's body.

The woman gazed at it for a second, then dropped it to the floor. Turning, she staggered toward the stairs, not looking back.

When she was gone, the doctor picked the locket up, wiped it clean, and dropped it in his pocket.

Chapter 1

*T*here was nothing about the First National Bank of Blackstone that Jules Hartwick didn't love. It was a passion that had begun when he was a very small boy and his father brought him down to the Bank for the first time. The memory of that first visit remained vividly sharp through the half century that had since passed. Even now Jules could recall the awe with which, as a child of three, he had first beheld the gleaming polished walnut of the desks and the great slabs of green-veined marble that topped all the counters.

But the brightest memory of that day—brighter than any other memory he had—was of the fascination that came over him when he'd seen the great door to the vault standing open, the intricate works of its locking mechanism clearly visible through a glass plate on the inside of the door. Every shiny piece of brass had captivated him, and over and over he'd begged Miss Schmidt, who had been his father's secretary right up until the day she died, to work the combination yet again so he could watch the tumblers fall, the levers work, and the huge pins that held the enormous door fast in its frame move in and out.

Half a century later, nothing had changed. The Bank (somehow, Jules always capitalized the word in his own mind) was no different now than it had been back then. Some of the marble showed a few chips, and there were some nicks in the walnut, but the tellers' cages were still fronted by the same flimsy brass grills that offered little in the way of security but a great deal in the way of atmosphere, and the huge vault door still stood open all day, allowing the Bank's customers to enjoy the beauty of its inner workings as much as Jules had on that long-ago day. Had he been forced to make a choice, Jules would have been hard put to say which he could live better without: his wife, or the Bank. Not that he'd thought of it much, until the last few weeks, when the auditors from the Federal Reserve had begun to raise disconcerting questions about the Bank's lending practices.

Now, as he sat in his office with Ed Becker, trying to concentrate on what his attorney was saying, his eyes fell on the desk calendar and the small notation in the box marking off this entire evening: "Dinner Party for Celeste and Andrew."

It was a party he'd been looking forward to for weeks, ever since Andrew Sterling had formally requested permission to marry his daughter. To ask for Celeste's hand in marriage was exactly the kind of endearingly anachronistic gesture Jules had come to expect of Andrew, who had been working at the Bank for almost five years, rising from teller to Chief Loan Officer not only on the merit of his work—which was considerable—but because Andrew, like Jules himself, preferred the old-fashioned way of banking.

"I know it's an idea the business schools don't approve of," he'd told Jules when they were discussing his promotion to the job he now held, "but I think there are far better ways to judge a man's worth than by his credit application."

It was precisely the philosophy upon which the Hartwicks had founded the Blackstone bank, and it confirmed Jules's judgment that Andrew, though only five years out of college, was perfectly qualified for the loan officer's job.

Now, the engagement of Andrew and Celeste was to be formally announced that night, though Jules suspected there were few people in Blackstone who weren't already aware of it. The bethrothal of his only daughter to this upstanding young man was the frosting on Jules's cake: a few more years and he might be able to consider the possibility of retirement, knowing the Bank would be in Andrew's capable hands, and that Andrew would be part of the family.

The continuity of First National of Blackstone would be ensured.

"Jules?"

Ed Becker's voice jerked the banker out of his reverie. When Jules shifted his eyes back from the calendar to his attorney, he saw the lawyer looking at him with a worried frown.

"Are you all right, Jules?"

"I'd be a lot righter if this audit were behind us," Hartwick replied, leaning forward. "Going to be some party tonight, isn't it? It should be one of the happiest nights of my life, and now I have this ruining it." He gestured to the stack of papers in front of them. The auditors were questioning nearly one hundred loans—and they were still at work. Jules could see no end in sight.

"But it's nothing more than a nuisance, when you get right down to it," Ed Becker said. "I've been over every one of these loans, and I haven't found anything illegal in any of them."

"And you won't," Jules Hartwick replied. He leaned forward in his chair, folding his hands on his desk. "Maybe," he said with a smile, "you were down there in Boston a little too long."

Becker grinned. "About five years too long, at least," he agreed. "But who knew I was going to get sick of— what did you used to call them?"

" 'Slimeballs,' " Jules Hartwick instantly replied. "And that's what they were, Ed. Murderers and rapists and gangsters. I'll never understand how—"

Ed Becker held up a hand in protest. "I know, I know.

But everyone deserves a defense, no matter what we might think of him. And I *did* get fed up with the whole thing, remember? I quit. I came back home to set up a nice quiet little practice, with nothing messier than the occasional divorce to deal with. But Jules, you probably know more than I do about business law. Sue me, or educate me. Why are you so worried about this? If there really isn't anything illegal about any of these loans, why are you making yourself sick over this?"

A brief and hollow chuckle emerged from Jules Hartwick. "If this weren't an independent bank, it wouldn't matter a damn," he said. "And maybe I've been wrong all these years. Maybe I should have sold out to one of the big interstate banks. God knows, it would have made Madeline and me far richer than we are today."

"I've seen your accounts, Jules, remember?" the lawyer put in archly. "You're not exactly suffering."

"And I haven't cashed out for a few hundred million like a lot of other bankers I won't name," Hartwick replied, the last trace of good humor vanishing from his voice. "I've always felt that this is more than just a bank, Ed. To me, and to my father, and to my grandfather, this bank has been a trust. We never thought it existed just for us. It's not just a business, like any other. This bank has always been part of the community. A vital, life-giving part. And to keep Blackstone alive over the years, I've made a lot of loans that a lot of other bankers might not have made. But I know the people I loan money to, Ed." He picked up one of the stacks of papers from his desk. "These are not bad loans."

The lawyer's eyes met those of the banker. "Then you have nothing to worry about, do you? It sounds like you should give the auditors what they're asking for before they start issuing subpoenas."

Hartwick's face paled slightly. "They're talking about subpoenas?"

"Of course they are."

Hartwick stood up. "I'll think about it," he said, but the reluctance was evident in his voice. The material the auditors wanted would show no criminal behavior on his part, but certainly it could be used by anyone who wished to make a case that his banking methods did not always conform to the standards that were currently considered prudent. That, he knew, could easily shift the balance on his Board of Directors, a majority of whom might finally be convinced that it was time that First National of Blackstone—like practically every other little bank in the country—sold out to one of the interstates.

If that happened, rich though he may be, he would no longer be in possession of the one thing he loved most.

Under no circumstances would Jules Hartwick allow that to happen.

He would find a way to keep his bank—and his life— intact.

Oliver Metcalf checked himself in the mirror one last time. It had been years since the last time he'd put on a necktie for dinner—only the very fanciest restaurants down in Boston and New York still required them—but Madeline Hartwick had been very specific. Tonight's dinner was going to be a throwback to days gone by—all the women were dressing, and all the men were expected to wear jackets and ties. Since he knew as well as everyone else that this was the night Celeste Hartwick and Andrew Sterling were announcing their engagement, he'd been more than happy to comply. His tie—the only one he owned—was more than a little out of date, and even his jacket—a tweed affair that had struck him as very "editorial" when he'd bought it—was starting to look just a bit shabby, now that it was entering its twentieth year. Still, it should all pass muster, and if Madeline began needling him about how a wife might be able to do wonders with his wardrobe, he'd simply smile and threaten to woo Celeste away from Andrew.

Leaving the house, he considered whether it was too cold to walk across the Asylum grounds and follow the path that wound through the woods down to the top of Harvard Street, where the Hartwicks lived. Then, remembering that he'd left the gift he'd found for Celeste and Andrew in his office, he abandoned any idea of walking and got into his car—a Volvo almost as ancient as his tweed jacket.

Five minutes later he slid the car into an empty slot in front of the *Blackstone Chronicle* and left the engine idling while he dashed inside to pick up the antique silver tray he'd come across last weekend, and which Lois Martin had insisted on rewrapping for him this afternoon. Peering into the large shopping bag where Lois left the tray, Oliver had to admit she'd done a far better job than he: the leftover red and green Christmas paper he'd used had been replaced with a silver and blue design printed with wedding bells, and no ragged edges showed anywhere, despite the cumbersome oval shape of the tray. Scribbling a quick thank-you note that Lois would find first thing in the morning, he relocked the office door, got back in his car, and headed toward Harvard Street. As he slowed to make at least a pretense of obeying the stop sign at the next corner, he saw Rebecca Morrison coming out of the library, and pulled over to the curb.

"Give you a lift?" he asked.

Rebecca seemed almost startled by the offer, but came over to the car. "Oh, Oliver, it's so far out of your way. I can walk."

"It's not out of my way at all," Oliver told her, reaching over and pushing the passenger door open. "I'm going up to the Hartwicks'."

Rebecca got into the car. "Are you going to the dinner?"

Oliver nodded. "You too?"

"Oh, no," Rebecca said quickly. "Aunt Martha says I mustn't go to things like that. She says I might say the wrong thing."

Oliver glanced over at Rebecca, whose face, softly illuminated by the streetlights, seemed utterly serene, despite the less than kind words she was repeating about herself.

"What does Martha want you to do?" Oliver asked. "Spend the rest of your life at home with her?"

"Aunt Martha's been very good to me since Mother and Father died," Rebecca replied. Though she had neatly sidestepped his question, he still failed to hear even the slightest note of discontent in her voice.

"You still have a life to live," Oliver said.

Rebecca's gentle smile returned. "I have a wonderful life, Oliver. I have my job at the library, and I have Aunt Martha for company. I count my blessings every day."

"Which is what Aunt Martha told you to do, right?" Oliver asked. Martha Ward, whose younger sister had been Rebecca's mother, had retreated deep into her religion on the day her husband moved out twenty-five years earlier. Her only child, Andrea, had left home on her eighteenth birthday. It had been just a few months after Andrea's departure that Rebecca's parents died in the automobile accident that nearly killed Rebecca as well. Aunt Martha had promptly taken her young niece in. And there, twelve years later, Rebecca remained.

There were even a few skeptical souls in Blackstone who thought that the accident had occurred in answer to Martha Ward's own prayers. "After all," Oliver once heard someone say, "first Fred Ward got out, and Andrea left as soon as she could. And since the accident, Rebecca hasn't been quite right in the head, so Martha has someone to pray over, and Rebecca has a place to live."

Except that Rebecca was perfectly all right "in the head," as far as Oliver could see. She was just a little quiet, and totally without guile. She said whatever came into her mind, which could sometimes be unnerving—at least for some people. Edna Burnham, for instance, had yet to recover from the day that Rebecca stopped her on the street and announced in front of three of Edna's best friends that she loved Edna's new wig. "It's so much better than that other one you used to wear," Rebecca assured her. "It always looked like a wig, and this one really does look real!"

Edna Burnham had never spoken to Rebecca again.

Oliver, who'd had the good fortune to be only ten feet away when the incident occurred, still hadn't stopped laughing about it.

And Rebecca, as utterly innocent as the sixteen-year-old she'd been on the day of the accident that killed her parents, had no idea why Edna Burnham was upset, or what amused Oliver so.

"But it *is* a wig, and it *does* look nice," she'd insisted.

Now, in reply to his question about her aunt, Rebecca told him exactly what she thought. "Aunt Martha means well," she said. "She can't help it if she's just a little bit odd."

"A little bit?" Oliver echoed.

Rebecca reddened slightly. "I'm the one everyone says is odd, Oliver."

"No you're not. You're just honest." He pulled the Volvo over to the curb in front of Martha Ward's house, next door to the Hartwicks'. "How about if you come to the dinner with me?" he suggested. "Madeline told me I could bring a date."

Rebecca's flush deepened and she shook her head. "I'm sure she didn't mean me, Oliver."

"I'm sure she didn't mean *not* you," Oliver replied. As

he got out and went around to open the door for her, he tried once more. "I didn't tell her I was coming alone. Why don't you just put on your prettiest dress and come with me?"

Rebecca shook her head again. "Oh, Oliver, I couldn't! Not in a million years. Besides, Aunt Martha says I make people uncomfortable, and she's right."

"You don't make me uncomfortable," Oliver retorted.

"You're sweet, Oliver," Rebecca said. Then, giving him a quick peck on the cheek, she added, "Have a good time, and tell Celeste and Andrew that I'm very happy for them."

Just then Martha Ward opened the front door of her house and stepped out onto the porch. "It's time for you to come in, Rebecca," she called. "I'm about to begin evening prayers."

"Yes, Aunt Martha." Rebecca turned away from Oliver and started up the walk toward her aunt's house.

Taking his gift out of the backseat of the Volvo, Oliver strode past the Ward house and turned up the Hartwicks' driveway. But as he neared the porte cochere he suddenly had the sense that he was being watched. Looking over his shoulder toward the Ward house, he saw that Rebecca still stood on the porch.

She was gazing at him, and even at this distance he could see the wistfulness in her face. But then he heard Martha Ward's voice call her once again. A moment later Rebecca disappeared into the house.

Suddenly wishing very much that he were not going to the party alone, Oliver mounted the Hartwicks' front steps and pressed the bell. Madeline Hartwick opened the door to greet him with a hug.

"Oliver," she said. "How wonderful." As she stepped back to let him in, her eyes flicked toward the house next door. "For a moment I thought you might be bringing poor Rebecca with you."

Oliver hesitated, then decided to be as truthful as

Rebecca would have been. "I asked her," he said. "But she turned me down." Though he tried to tell himself he was mistaken, Oliver was certain he saw a look of relief pass over Madeline Hartwick's perfectly made-up face.

Chapter 2

Jules Hartwick leaned back in his chair and gave Madeline an almost imperceptible nod, the signal that it was time for Madeline to let her toe touch the button on the floor beneath her end of the dining room table. It would summon the maid who had been hired for the evening to clear the dessert plates while the butler—also hired only for the evening—served the port. The dining room had always been one of Jules's favorite rooms in the house he'd grown up in, and into which he and Madeline had moved a decade ago, after his father, widowed for fifteen years, retired to a condo complex in Scottsdale. "It's perfect for me," the elder Hartwick had declared. "Full of Republicans and divorcées with enough money that they don't need mine."

Like all the rooms in the house, the dining room was immense, but so perfectly proportioned that it didn't seem overly large even when the party, like tonight's, was small. A pair of chandeliers glittered from its high-beamed ceiling, and the plaster walls above the mahogany wainscoting were hung with tapestries so luxuriously heavy that even the largest parties never seemed overly noisy. One wall was dominated by an immense fireplace, in which three large logs blazed merrily, and there was a sideboard built into the opposite wall, which served perfectly for the informal buffets that were this generation's preferred way to serve. "So much less ostentatious than the staff Jules's grandfather used to have," Madeline was fond of explaining, never mentioning that economics might have something to do with the scaled-back festivities that were now the rule in the house. Still, every now and then—on occasions such as tonight's—Jules liked to hire a full staff and do his best to roll the calendar back a generation or two. Tonight, he decided, had been a total success.

All the men save Oliver Metcalf had worn black tie, and, since no one had expected Oliver to appear in anything except his old tweed jacket, he didn't seem the least bit out of place. The women were resplendent in their evening dresses, and while Madeline looked even more elegant than usual in a long black sheath set off by a single strand of perfect pearls, Celeste had stolen the limelight in a flow of emerald green velvet that was a perfect complement to her auburn hair. She wore a single stunning piece of jewelry: a small spray of emeralds set in gold that had belonged to Jules's mother glittered near the heart-shaped neckline of her dress. Seated opposite her at the center of the long table, Andrew Sterling, Jules observed, had been unable to keep his eyes off his fiancée for more than a few seconds at a time. Which, Jules reflected, was exactly as it should be.

The rest of the party—all except one—seemed to be nearly as happy as Celeste and Andrew. Aside from Oliver Metcalf and Ed and Bonnie Becker, Madeline had invited Harvey Connally—"to represent the older generation, which I think gives a nice continuity to things"— and included Edna Burnham as the old man's dinner partner. She'd also managed to persuade Bill McGuire to come out for the first time since Elizabeth's death, and included Lois Martin as part of her ongoing plan to match Oliver with his assistant outside the office as well as in. When Jules suggested that perhaps Oliver and Lois spent enough time together at the *Chronicle*, Madeline had given him the kind of wifely look that informed him very clearly that while his banking skills might be excellent, he knew nothing about matchmaking.

"Lois and Oliver are perfect for each other," she'd said. "They just don't know it."

Though Jules suspected Oliver's interest in Lois ended at the office door, he'd kept his own counsel, just as he had when his wife decided to invite Janice Anderson to fill the seat across from Bill McGuire. Not that Jules didn't like Janice. With a perfect combination of business acumen and a winning personality that made her immediately seem like everyone's best friend, Janice had built her antique shop into a business strong enough to bring people to Blackstone from hundreds of miles around. It had been Bill McGuire who convinced her to move her shop into Blackstone Center as soon as the new complex was completed.

Tonight, though, even Janice's sunny disposition didn't seem to be working on Bill. The poor man appeared to Jules to have taken on an unhealthy gauntness since Elizabeth's death a month ago. Still, he seemed glad he'd come, and on balance, Jules decided that Madeline had been right: if anyone would be able to take Bill's mind off his troubles for a little while, it would be Janice.

"Shall we take the port into the library?" Madeline asked as the butler finished filling the glasses. "We found something in the attic last week that we've been dying to show off."

"So that accounts for the library door being closed when we came in," Oliver Metcalf said. He'd risen to his feet to help Lois Martin move her heavy chair back from the huge marble-topped table. The guests all followed their hostess out of the dining room and through the reception room where they'd gathered for drinks—then across the great entry hall that was dominated by a sweeping staircase that led to the second floor mezzanine.

While the dining room had always been Jules's favorite, the library was Madeline's. Its ceiling vaulted up two full floors, and the walls, save for the areas where family portraits hung, were lined with floor-to-ceiling bookcases, their upper shelves so high that to reach them required the use of a wheeled ladder hung from a polished brass guide rail at the top. For Madeline, though, the bookcases were not the room's most distinguishing feature.

Directly above the double doors through which she had just led her guests was a minstrel's gallery large enough to hold a string quartet, and paneled in mahogany linenfold. Tonight, in honor of her daughter's engagement, she had hired a quartet, which was already playing softly when the company entered the room.

"Fabulous," Janice Anderson told Madeline. "It's like going back in time. I truly feel as if I've stepped into another century."

"Just wait till you see what we found in the attic— something amazing from yesteryear," Madeline promised her. "When the Center is done, of course we're going to donate it, but for now we just couldn't resist hanging it in here."

She led them to the far end of the room, where a picture, covered by a black cloth, had been hung. When everyone had gathered around, she signaled to Jules to lower the lights until the only illumination in the room was provided by a spotlight on the picture. As an expectant hush fell, Madeline pulled a cord and the picture's covering fell away.

From an ornately gilded frame, an aristocratic woman of perhaps forty gazed down on the room. She was wearing a dark blue dress of shimmering silk. Despite her elegant bearing and expensive clothing, her eyes gazed out from the canvas accusingly, as if she had resented having her portrait painted. Her hair was pulled severely back from her high forehead, apparently done in an elaborate twist at the back, and she stood beside a chair. The fingers of one hand clutched tightly to the back of the chair, while the other hand, though hanging at her side, appeared to be clenched in a fist.

"It's your mother, isn't it, Jules?" Janice Anderson asked. "But what a strange costume to have a portrait painted in. What is that she's wearing?" Indeed, though the woman in the portrait wore an elegant blue dress, over it was a pale gray apronlike affair that looked to be made of a heavy cotton material.

"We think it's her uniform from the Asylum," Jules replied. His eyes were fixed on the portrait, and he was frowning deeply, as if trying to figure out why his mother appeared so angry. "Apparently she volunteered her services as a Gray Lady at some point. Oddly enough, though, I don't ever remember seeing her wear that uniform. Until last week, I had no idea the portrait even existed." He turned to Oliver. "Do you remember ever seeing my mother like that?"

But Oliver Metcalf wasn't listening. The instant he'd seen the picture, a sharp pain flashed through his head, and a vision appeared in his mind.

The boy, naked and terrified, is shivering in the huge room.

His thin arms are wrapped around his body in a vain effort to keep himself warm.

The man appears, and the boy shrinks away from him, but there is no escape. The man holds a sheet in his hands—a wet sheet—and though the boy tries to slip past the man and dash from the room, the man catches him in the sheet as easily as a butterfly is caught in a net. In an instant the icy cold sheet engulfs the boy, who opens his mouth to scream—

* * *

"Oliver?" Jules Hartwick said again. "Oliver, is something wrong?"

Abruptly, the strange vision vanished. His headache eased and Oliver managed a small smile. "I'm fine," he assured Jules. He looked up at the portrait once more, half expecting the pounding pain behind his eyes to return, but this time there was nothing. Just the painting of Jules's mother in the uniform the volunteers at the Asylum had worn decades ago. Vaguely, he remembered reading somewhere how it had once been the fashion for people of means to have portraits done that reflected their professions or avocations. The costume, he ventured a guess to Jules, was Mrs. Hartwick's way of proclaiming her service to the town.

"I suppose so," Jules agreed. "But the weird thing is, I don't even remember Mother volunteering. But she must have, mustn't she?" He glanced up at the portrait again, then shook his head. "Easy to see why she put it up in the attic the minute it was done. But I think it could be kind of fun up at the Center, don't you? Maybe we can find pictures of some of the other women, and make it the centerpiece of an exhibit. Call it 'The Do-Gooders of Blackstone' or something."

"Jules!" Madeline exclaimed. "Those women took their work very seriously, and did a lot of good."

"I'm sure they did," Jules said. "But you still have to admit that Mother looks pretty unhappy about the whole thing."

"I'm sure her expression had nothing to do with her work at the Asylum," Madeline insisted. But then she relented, and a smile played around her lips. "Actually, she looks almost as disapproving as she did the day you married me."

"Well, she got over that," Jules said, slipping an arm

around his wife as the quartet in the minstrel's gallery began playing a waltz. "Marrying you was still the best thing I ever did." Pulling Madeline close, he swept her across the library floor in a few graceful steps. A moment later the rest of the party had joined in the dancing.

The portrait on the wall, and Jules's mother, were quickly forgotten as the party swirled on.

Rebecca felt as though she were going to suffocate.

The air in the room was thick with smoke from the rows of votive candles that lined the altar, and heavy with the choking perfume of incense.

The droning of Gregorian chants didn't quite drown out the sound of her aunt's voice as Martha Ward, on her knees next to Rebecca, mumbled her supplications and fingered the rosary beads she held in trembling hands.

An agonized Christ gazed down from the cross on the wall above the altar. Rebecca cringed as her eyes fixed on the trickle of painted blood oozing from the spear wound in his side. Feeling his pain as vividly as he must have felt it himself, she quickly moved her gaze away from the suffering figure.

It had been nearly two hours since they finished supper, and her aunt had led her here to beg forgiveness for the thoughts she had harbored during the meal. But how could Aunt Martha have known what crossed her mind when she caught a glimpse of the party going on next door? She'd barely had time to think at all before Aunt Martha, seeing her gazing out the kitchen window at the Hartwicks' brightly lit house, had pulled the blinds down, taken her by the arm, and marched her into this downstairs room that served as her aunt's private chapel.

It wasn't really a chapel at all, of course. Originally it had been her uncle's den, but shortly after Fred Ward left, her aunt had converted it into a place of worship, sealing the windows that once looked out on a lovely garden with curtains so heavy that no light penetrated them. Where there had once been a fireplace—which on a night like this might have blazed with crackling logs—there was now an ornate fifteenth-century Italian altar that Janice Anderson had discovered somewhere in Italy. Venice, maybe? Probably. Rebecca had found a book in the town library with a picture that showed a piece very much like Aunt Martha's. For all Rebecca knew, it might be the very same one.

The pungent aroma of incense and smoking candles filled Rebecca's nostrils and stung her eyes. Finally, when she was certain that her aunt was so far lost in her prayers that she wouldn't notice her absence, Rebecca eased herself onto the hard wooden bench, the only furniture in the room except for the altar and the prie-dieu upon which her aunt often knelt for hours at a time. As soon as her knees stopped hurting enough that she trusted them to hold her, she slipped out of the chapel and up to her room.

After changing into her nightgown, Rebecca was about to turn back the coverlet on her bed when she heard the sound of an automobile engine starting, and went to the window. It had begun to snow, and the night had turned brilliant in the glow of the streetlights. Next door, the party was breaking up, and Rebecca easily recognized all the guests as they said their good-nights to the Hartwicks. Maybe, after all, she should have accepted Oliver's invitation, she reflected. But it wouldn't have been right—Madeline Hartwick meticulously planned every detail of her dinners, and the last thing she'd have been able to cope with would be the last-minute appearance of an uninvited guest.

Still, it would have been nice to have gone, and spent an evening with smiling people, and pretend that they were her friends.

That's unkind, Rebecca told herself. Besides, Oliver *is* your friend!

As if he'd heard her thought, Oliver, who was seeing Lois Martin into her car, suddenly looked up. Smiling, he waved to Rebecca, and she waved back. But then, as first Janice Anderson and then Bill McGuire followed Oliver's glance to see who he was waving at, she felt a hot surge of embarrassment and quickly stepped back from the window. If Aunt Martha caught her, she would spend the next whole week repenting in the chapel!

Going to bed, Rebecca turned off the light and lay in the darkness, enjoying the glow from beyond her window and the shadow play on her ceiling and walls. Soon she drifted into a sleep so light that when she came awake an hour later she was barely aware that she'd been sleeping at all. She listened to the utter silence in the house. No chants drifted up from downstairs, which meant that her aunt, too, had gone to bed. It must be very late, Rebecca thought.

What had awakened her?

She listened even more intently, but if it had been a noise that had startled her awake, it wasn't repeated.

Nor had any strange shadows appeared on her ceiling.

Yet something had disturbed her sleep. After several minutes, Rebecca slipped out of her bed and went to the window, this time leaving the light off.

The night was filled with snow. It swirled around the streetlights, burying the cars in the street and covering the naked trees with a glistening coat of white. Next door, the Hartwicks' house had all but vanished, appearing as nothing more than an indistinct shape, though a few of its windows still glowed with a golden light that made Rebecca think of long-ago winter evenings when her parents had still been alive and her family snuggled in front of the fireplace and—

A sudden movement cut into her reverie, and then, out of the shadows of the Hartwicks' porte cochere, a dark figure appeared. As Rebecca watched, it went quickly down the driveway to the sidewalk, crossed the street, then vanished into the snowstorm.

Save for the footprints in the snow, Rebecca wouldn't have been sure she'd seen it at all. Indeed, by the time she went back to bed a few moments later, even the footprints had all but disappeared.

As the grandfather clock in the Hartwicks' entry hall struck the first note of the Westminster chime, the four people in the smallest of the downstairs rooms fell silent. The big, encased timepiece in the entry hall was only the first of a dozen clocks in the house that would strike one after the other, filling the house with the sounds of gongs and chimes of every imaginable pitch. Now, as the clocks Jules had collected from every corner of the world began marking the midnight hour, Madeline slipped her hand into her husband's, and Celeste, on the sofa opposite her parents, snuggled closer against Andrew. None of them spoke again until the last chime had finally died away.

"I always thought the clocks would drive me crazy," Madeline mused. "But now I don't know what I'd do without them."

"Well, you'll never have to," Jules assured her. "Actually, I've got a line on an old German cuckoo that I think might go nicely on the landing."

"A *cuckoo*?" Celeste echoed. "Dad, they're so corny!"

"I think a cuckoo would be fun," Jules said. Then, sensing that not only was Madeline going to take Celeste's side, but Andrew was too, he relented. "All right, suppose I put it in my den?" he offered in compromise. "They're not *that* bad, you know!"

"They are too, and you know it," Madeline replied. Rising from the sofa with a brisk movement that conveyed to Andrew that the evening was at an end, she picked up Jules's port glass, despite that fact that half an inch of the ruby fluid remained in it.

"I guess I'm done with that," Jules observed.

"I guess you are," Madeline agreed. She leaned down to give him an affectionate kiss on his forehead.

"I hope Celeste takes as good care of me as Mrs. Hartwick does of you, sir," Andrew Sterling said a few minutes later as he and Jules stepped out into the snowy night.

"I'm sure she will," Jules replied, throwing an arm around his prospective son-in-law's shoulders. "Or at least she'll come close. Nobody could take as good care of a man as Madeline takes of me." His voice took on what seemed to Andrew an oddly wistful note. "I've been a very lucky man. I suppose I should count my blessings."

They were at Andrew's car now, and as Andrew brushed the snow off its windshield, he glanced quizzically at the older man. "Is something wrong, sir?"

For a moment Jules was tempted to mention the audit, then decided against it. He'd managed to get through the entire evening without talking at all about his worries at the Bank, and he certainly had no intention of burdening Andrew with them now. None of it, after all, was this young man's fault. If there was blame to be borne, Jules thought, he would certainly bear it himself. "Nothing at all," he assured Andrew. "It's just been a wonderful evening, and I am, indeed, a very lucky man. I have Madeline, and Celeste, and I couldn't ask for a better son-in-law. Get a good night's sleep, and I'll see you in the morning."

As Andrew drove away, Jules swung the big wrought-iron gate across the driveway, then started back toward the house. But coming abreast of Madeline's car, still free of snow under the porte cochere, he noticed that the driver's door was slightly ajar. As he pulled it open in preparation for closing it all the way, the interior light flashed on, revealing a small package, neatly wrapped, sitting on the front seat. Frowning, he picked it up, closed the car door tight, and continued back into the house. Pausing in the entry hall, he turned the package over, looking for some clue as to where it had come from.

There was nothing.

It was simply a small box, wrapped in pink paper and tied with a silver ribbon.

Had Madeline bought it as a gift for him?

The pink paper was enough to put that idea out of his mind. Nor was his wife the kind of woman to leave a gift sitting in her car, not even concealed in a bag.

As he stood at the foot of the stairs, Jules realized that Madeline had not bought the gift at all.

No, she was the intended recipient of the gift, not the giver.

But who was it from? And why had it been left in Madeline's car?

Without thinking, Jules found himself pulling the ribbon from the package, and then the paper. A moment later he'd opened the box itself and found himself looking at a small silver locket.

A locket in the shape of a heart.

His fingers shaking, he picked the locket up and opened it.

Where a picture might have been—should have been—there was nothing.

Nothing, save a lock of hair.

Closing the locket, Jules clutched it in his hand and gazed up the stairs toward the floor above. Suddenly an image came into his mind.

An image of Madeline.

Madeline, whom he'd loved for more than a quarter of a century.

Whom he'd thought loved him too.

But now, in his mind's eye, he could see her clearly.

And she was in the arms of another man.

As he put the locket in his coat pocket, Jules Hartwick felt the foundations of his world starting to crumble.

Chapter 3

"*M*other, for heaven's sake, look outside!" Celeste Hartwick said as she came into the breakfast room the next morning and poured herself a cup of coffee from the big silver carafe on the table. "It's fabulous!"

But even with her daughter's urging, Madeline barely glanced at the sparkling snowscape that lay beyond the French doors. Every twig of every tree and bush was laden with a thick layer of white, and the blanket of snow that covered the lawns and paths was unbroken save for a single set of bird tracks, apparently made by the cardinal that was now perched on a branch of the big chestnut tree just outside the window, providing the only splash of color in the monochromatic scene.

"Okay, Mother," Celeste said, seating herself in the chair opposite Madeline. "Obviously something's wrong. What is it?"

Madeline pursed her lips, wondering exactly what to say to Celeste, for the truth was that though something was, indeed, wrong, even she herself had no idea what it was. It had begun last night, when Jules had come up after seeing Andrew out and closing the gate. When he entered their bedroom, he'd barely looked at her, and when she'd spoken to him, asking if something was wrong, he positively glared at her and informed her that if something were wrong, she would know it better than he. Then, before she could say another word, he'd disappeared into his dressing room and not come out for nearly thirty minutes. When he finally appeared in his pajamas, he slid into bed beside her, then turned out the light without so much as a good-night, let alone a kiss. Having picked up very clearly that he was in no mood to communicate with her, she'd decided that rather than make this unexpected situation worse by trying to drag the problem out of him in the middle of the night, she would let it go until morning. She'd managed to sleep— at least sporadically—but every time she awakened, she could feel him lying stiffly next to her. Though she'd known by the rhythm of his breathing that he was as wide awake as she, he made no response when she'd spoken to him.

Now she asked her daughter, "Were you still up when your father came in last night?"

Celeste nodded. "But I didn't see him. I heard him come up, but I was in my room. Did something happen?"

"I don't know—" Madeline began. "I mean, I think something must have happened, but I haven't the slightest idea what. It was the most peculiar thing, Celeste. When your father came to bed last night, he was barely speaking to me. He—"

"Do you tell *everyone* what happens in our bed, Madeline?"

Recoiling from his words as if she'd been slapped, Madeline's whole body jerked reflexively. Coffee splashed from her cup onto the table. As Celeste quickly blotted the spill with a paper napkin, Madeline shakily set the cup back onto its saucer. "For heaven's sake, Jules, will you please tell me what's going on? Did Andrew say something last night that upset you?"

Andrew, Jules thought. His hand, shoved deep in his pocket, closed on the locket, its metal so hot it seemed to burn into his palm. Could it be Andrew? But Andrew was in love with Celeste, not with Madeline. Or was he? It wouldn't be the first time a young man had fallen in love with a woman old enough to be his mother. "Why do you ask?" he said aloud.

The shock of his words giving way to impatience, Madeline picked her napkin off her lap and began folding it slowly and neatly, pressing each crease flat with the palm of her right hand. It was an unconscious gesture that both Celeste and Jules had long ago learned to recognize as a sign that Madeline was annoyed. Though Celeste threw her father a warning glance, it seemed to have no effect whatsoever.

"I ask," Madeline said in a perfectly controlled voice that made Celeste brace herself for a breaking storm, "because I do not know what is going on. When I asked you last night if something was wrong, you said I would know better than you. Now you are implying that I am in the habit of discussing our bedroom activities with other people, which is something you are well aware that I would never do. If something is wrong, Jules, please tell me what it is."

Jules's eyes flicked suspiciously from his wife to his daughter. How much did Celeste know? Probably everything—didn't mothers always confide in their daughters? "What's his name, Madeline?" he finally asked. "Or should I ask Celeste?" He turned to his daughter. "Who is it, Celeste? Is it someone I know?"

Celeste glanced uncertainly from one of her parents to the other. What on earth was going on? Last night, when she'd gone up to bed, everything had been perfect. What could have happened? "I'm sorry, Daddy," she began. "I don't—"

"Oh, please, Celeste," Jules said, his voice carrying a knife edge she'd never heard before. "I'm not a fool, you know. I know all about your mother's affair."

Now it was Celeste whose coffee splashed across the table as her cup fell from her hand. "Her *what*?" she asked. But before Jules could say anything more, she'd turned to her mother. "He thinks you're having an affair?"

Madeline was on her feet, her eyes glittering with anger. "Tell me what this is all about, Jules," she demanded. "Where on earth did you get such an idea? Did Andrew say something last night to put such a ridiculous idea into your head?"

"Don't be stupid, Madeline," Jules cut in. "Andrew didn't say anything." His hand, still in his pocket, squeezed the locket so tightly he felt its filigree digging into his flesh. "He'd be the last person to say anything, wouldn't he?"

Now Celeste was on her feet too. "Stop it, Daddy. How can you even think such a thing? Andrew and Mother? That's the most disgusting thing I've ever heard!"

Jules's eyes, narrowed to little more than slits, darted back and forth between his wife and his daughter. "You didn't think I'd find out, did you?" he asked. "But I did find out, didn't I? And I'm damn well going to find out all the rest of it too." Leaving Madeline and Celeste staring speechlessly after him, Jules Hartwick turned and strode out of the breakfast room.

"It's the Devil's work!"

Martha Ward's words were uttered with such sharpness that they made Rebecca flinch and instinctively wonder what sin she might have committed this time. But then the wave of guilt receded as she realized the words hadn't been directed toward her at all. Martha was on the telephone, and this time, at least, it was her cousin Andrea who was the recipient of her aunt's lecture.

"I warned you," Martha continued, holding the phone in her left hand as she used her right to gesture to Rebecca to pour her another cup of coffee. "When I first met that man, I recognized him for what he was. Didn't I say, 'Andrea, that man has the face of Satan'? Of course I did, whether you want to remember it or not." She fell silent for a moment, then clucked her tongue in a manner not so much sympathetic as disapproving. "You must go to church, Andrea," she admonished. "You must go and pray for your immortal soul, and beg for forgiveness. And the next time, perhaps you'll recognize the Devil when you see him!"

Hanging up the phone, Martha Ward scooped three teaspoonsful of sugar into her coffee, added some cream, then sighed as she sipped at the steaming mixture. "I think this time I truly put the fear of the Devil into that child," she declared. "But it's true, Rebecca. The first time I saw Gary Fletcher, I warned Andrea about him. I told her never to bring him to this house again. I am a woman of the Church, and I will not countenance evil in my presence."

"But how can you recognize Satan, Aunt Martha?" Rebecca asked, an image still fresh in her mind of the dark figure she'd seen in the snowstorm last night.

"You know him when you see him," Martha stated. "It doesn't matter what guise he takes on, a person of virtue can always recognize the Devil."

"But what does he look like?" Rebecca pressed. "How would I *know* if I've seen him?"

Martha Ward set her coffee cup down and regarded her niece suspiciously. There was a lot of her father in Rebecca, and Martha Ward had never approved of the man her sister, Margaret, had married, any more than she did of the man her daughter, Andrea, was living with. Mick Morrison, as far as Martha had been concerned, was evil incarnate. It had always been her firm belief that the accident that killed both him and her sister was nothing short of God's retribution for Mick Morrison's sinning ways, and Meg's countenancing those sins. Rebecca, she assumed, had been spared her life because she was so young, but there was still more of Mick Morrison in her niece than Martha would have preferred. The vigilance required to prevent Rebecca from giving in to the wickedness inherited from her father was just one more of the crosses she'd been called upon to bear. Martha sighed heavily. "Just what are you trying to get at, Rebecca?"

"I saw something last night," her niece replied. "It was after the Hartwicks' party." She described the figure she'd seen emerging from the porte cochere next door. "And he just vanished into the snow," she finished. "It was almost like he hadn't been there at all."

Martha Ward's face pinched in disapproval of her niece's recitation. "Perhaps he wasn't there, Rebecca," she suggested. "Perhaps you merely invented this mysterious person to justify having been spying on our neighbors. The Hartwicks are good, decent people, and they don't need you peeping at them in the middle of the night. I suggest you go to the chapel and say three Hail Marys in repentance. And as for the Devil," she added pointedly as Rebecca hurried to obey her order, "I think you should look very carefully at Oliver Metcalf."

There, she told herself as Rebecca left the room. I've done my duty, and if anything bad happens to her, it's nobody's fault but her own.

Jules Hartwick could feel them watching him.

It started the moment he left the house. Even as he walked down the driveway to the sidewalk, he'd known that Martha Ward and Rebecca Morrison were watching. Twice he turned to glare accusingly at them, but both times they were too quick for him, stepping back from their windows before he caught even a glimpse of them.

But they weren't fooling him—he knew they were there!

Just as he knew the rest of his neighbors on Harvard Street were watching him as he made his way down the hill toward Main. How long had they been watching him? Years, probably. And he knew why.

They were all his enemies.

He understood it all this morning with a clarity he'd never had before.

They knew about the problems at the Bank.

They knew about the affair Madeline was having.

And they were laughing at him, laughing at his humiliation, laughing at the indignity, the dishonor that was about to befall him. But he wouldn't give them the satisfaction of seeing him suffer, wouldn't even let them know he'd finally caught on to them. He held his head high as he turned onto Main Street and walked right past the Red Hen Diner, where half the leading businessmen in Blackstone gathered every morning for coffee.

Their real purpose, of course, was to plot against him, to plan the downfall of not only his bank, but himself as well. And they'd been clever, going so far as to ask him to join their group in order to keep him from guessing its true purpose. But this morning, finally, he understood why some of them were always already there when he arrived, and others always lingered after he left. They were talking about him, whispering to each other behind his back, plotting every detail of his downfall.

But he wouldn't let it happen.

Now that he knew what they were doing, he could out-maneuver them. He'd always been smarter than the rest of them, and that was another reason they hated him.

Well, they might hate him, but they wouldn't beat him!

Now, as he stepped through the door of the Bank, he could feel the whole staff watching him, even though they were pretending not to be.

The tellers were behind their windows, ostensibly

counting their cash drawers, but he knew they were secretly observing him, following every step he took as he started toward his office at the back of the Bank in the corner next to the vault.

But it wasn't just the tellers who were watching him. The guards were all following his progress too. The hairs on the back of his neck were standing on end, and he felt a shiver pass through him that didn't release him from its cold grip until he was inside his office and had closed the door behind him. He leaned against it for a moment, waiting for the tension that had been building inside him from the moment he left the house to ease.

Now, for the first time, he felt his heart pounding.

Had Madeline put something in his coffee this morning? No, he'd fooled her and hadn't had any coffee.

Finally moving away from the door, he went to his desk and dropped into the big chair that had been his father's and grandfather's before him. He was about to press the button on the intercom and ask Ellen Golding to bring him a cup of coffee, but quickly thought better of it. Whatever was going on at the Bank—and it was clear now that the Federal Reserve audit was only part of a much larger conspiracy—surely they would have recruited Ellen at the very beginning.

Better to get his own coffee before that sneaking bitch could doctor it!

Stepping out of the office, he went to the coffeepot Ellen always kept on the credenza that contained all his files and started to pour himself a cup.

"Why didn't you call me, Mr. Hartwick?" Ellen asked. "I could have done that for you."

He'd been right! She would have put something in it. Should he fire her right now? Better not to let them know he was on to them yet. "I'm not totally helpless, Ellen," he said. "Besides, isn't asking your secretary to bring you coffee considered grounds for a lawsuit these days?"

Ellen Golding stared at her boss. What on earth was he talking about? She'd been his secretary for nearly ten years, and brought him a cup of coffee every single morning. It was part of her job, for God's sake! "Are you all right, Mr. Hartwick?"

"Don't I look all right?" Jules shot back. "Do I look like something's wrong with me? Well, I can assure you, Miss Golding, that nothing is wrong with me, and nothing is *going* to be wrong with me, no matter how clever you might think you are." Taking the cup of coffee with him, he retreated to his office, closing the door behind him once more. Back at his desk, he took a sip of the coffee.

It had a bitter flavor to it that instantly put him on his guard. Had Ellen put something in the pot?

He pushed the cup aside.

Suddenly, the feeling of being watched swept over him again. But how? He was alone in his office.

Wasn't he?

What if someone was hiding in his private bathroom? Rising abruptly, he moved to the bathroom door, listened for a moment, then pulled the door open.

Empty.

Or was it?

What about the shower?

His heart pounding harder, he crossed the tile floor.

The shower curtain was closed, but he could almost feel the presence behind it.

Who?

In a movement so quick it surprised even himself, he reached out and snatched the curtain aside with so much force that three of its rings tore loose from the plastic fabric.

The stall was empty. Venting his frustration by jerking the rest of the curtain loose, he left it crumpled on the bathroom floor and went back to his office. And the moment he was back inside the paneled room, he knew where the watchers were hiding.

The security cameras!

There were two of them, set up six years ago not because Jules thought them necessary but because the insurance company had offered a reduction in premiums if they were installed. Now, however, he understood the real reason the insurance company had wanted the cameras put in. It wasn't to protect security at all.

It was so they could spy on him!

He picked up the phone and punched in the extension for his executive vice-president. "I want the security cameras in my office turned off," he said without so much as a good morning.

"I beg your pardon?" Melissa Holloway asked.

"You heard me!" Jules snapped. "I want the cameras in my office off right now, and taken out completely by lunchtime!" Slamming the phone back onto its cradle, he glowered up at the mechanical eye that stared at him from the corner. Then, unable to bear being watched a moment longer, Jules Hartwick left his desk once more.

Ten seconds later, having failed for the first time in his life to respond to every employee who spoke to him, he was on his way home.

Once again his right hand was buried deep in his pocket, clutching the locket.

Chapter 4

Ed Becker knew something had gone wrong the moment he walked into the bank that morning. Though there was only one customer at the tellers' windows, there were whispered conversations going on everywhere, nearly all of which quickly died away as people became aware of his presence. At first he assumed that something had happened with regard to the audit, but when he glanced into the glass-fronted conference room in which the audit was taking place, the man and two women from the Fed were hard at work, each of them poring over a thick stack of computer printouts, just as they'd been doing for weeks. He was about to head for Jules Hartwick's office when Melissa Holloway beckoned him to her desk.

"Was Mr. Hartwick all right last night?" she asked.

Ed Becker felt eyes watching him from every direction. "He was fine," he assured the executive vice-president. "But I assume from the question that he isn't this morning. Is he in his office?"

Melissa Holloway shook her head. "He was here for about ten minutes," she told him. "First, he almost bit Ellen Golding's head off and then he called me and ordered—"

"Ordered?" Ed Becker echoed. In all the years he'd known Jules, he'd never heard the banker utter any instruction in terms that could be construed as an "order." Countless times he had heard Jules request that things he needed be done, but Ed had never witnessed even a hint of the kind of authoritarian behavior implied by the word Melissa Holloway had used.

Melissa shrugged helplessly. "I know. It's not like Mr. Hartwick at all. But he ordered me to turn off the security cameras in his office—immediately—and have them completely removed by noon."

Had it not been for the pallor of Melissa's complexion and the worry in her expression, Ed Becker would have suspected she was pulling his leg. Obviously, though, she wasn't. "And then he left?"

Melissa nodded. "Without speaking to anyone. And he didn't speak to anyone when he came in either. Ed, he *always* speaks to everyone. It might not be more than a word or two, but he always has at least a 'good morning.' But not today. It was like—" She hesitated, floundering, then shook her head. "I don't know what it was like. It was crazy!"

"What about the auditors?" Ed asked, lowering his voice so it would carry no farther than Melissa's ears. "Could they have found something that might have upset him?"

"It's the first thing I thought of, but none of them even said hello to him. I was hoping maybe you might know what's going on."

Before Ed could say anything else, Andrew Sterling came over, his face red, a vein throbbing in his forehead. "Do you have any idea what the hell is going on with Jules?" he demanded, his voice harsh.

Ed Becker braced himself. "What did he say to you?"

"Nothing. But I just got a call from Celeste. For some reason her father seems to think that—" He fell silent for a moment, and it was apparent to both Ed Becker and Melissa Holloway that he had to force himself to continue. "He seems to have gotten the idea in his head that Celeste's mother is having an affair."

"Madeline?" Ed Becker gasped. "Come on, Andrew. You've got to be kidding!"

"I wish I were. But it gets worse. It seems he thinks *I'm* the person she's—" Again he went silent. This time, it was apparent Andrew wasn't going to be able to finish the sentence at all.

"Jules actually *said* that?" Ed asked. When Andrew made no answer, Ed took a deep breath, then slowly let it out. "I guess I'd better go up there and see what's going on."

The gate at the foot of the Hartwicks' driveway stood open. Madeline's car was gone, so Ed pulled his Buick under the porte cochere and strode up the steps. Ringing the bell, he shivered in the cold as he waited for Jules Hartwick to open the door. When the banker hadn't appeared after a full minute went by, he rang the bell again. When there was still no response, Ed went back to the Buick, pulled his winter coat out of the backseat and put it on, then went around to the back of the house.

Peering through one of the windows in the garage, he saw that Jules's black Lincoln Town Car was inside. Of course, that didn't necessarily mean that Jules himself was at home; like almost everyone in Blackstone, Jules walked to work unless the weather was truly horrible, and it had been Melissa Holloway's impression that Jules had, indeed, walked down to the bank that morning. Mounting the steps to the large glassed-in back porch, Ed let himself though the storm door, then tried the back door.

Locked.

He looked for a bell, found none, and knocked loudly.

There was no more response from within than there'd been at the front door a few minutes earlier.

Leaving the back porch, Ed circled the house to the other side, past the breakfast room, then moved onto the broad terrace. There, sets of French doors, one at each end, led into the library and the large formal living room. He cupped his hands around his eyes in an attempt to peer into the shadowy rooms beyond the doors, but the shirred material covering the panes defeated his efforts.

He moved on around the house, his shoes now squishing with icy water and the bottoms of his pants heavy with snow. Rounding the far corner, he came to the protrusion next to the library that housed Jules Hartwick's den.

Heavy drapes had been drawn over both the windows flanking the small fireplace that was the room's dominant feature, and the windows were far too high for Ed to have seen through them even had curtains not covered them. He made his way around to the front door again and jabbed the bell three more times, but got no more response than before. Finally giving up, he returned to his car, got in, and started the engine. It wasn't until he'd reached the street that he saw it: smoke curling from the chimney that vented the fireplace in Jules Hartwick's den.

Ed Becker pulled back into the driveway, then sat staring at the drifting smoke. The den, he knew, was the one room in the house that neither Madeline nor Celeste ever went into. "I don't have even the slightest desire to go in there," he remembered Madeline saying a few months ago. "He has it exactly the way he wants it, and if he doesn't mind the stink of those awful cigars he thinks I don't know he smokes, so be it. He keeps the door shut, and I stay out. Which is fine, since I think we all need a place to go when we want to hide. I have my dressing room, and Jules has his den, and we share the rest of the house. It works perfectly."

And it also meant that if there was a fire on the den's hearth, then Jules was there.

Ed turned on his cellular phone and dialed Jules's private number. On the fourth ring the answering machine came on. He listened patiently as Jules's recorded greeting played through. When the machine beeped, Ed began talking. "You might as well pick up the phone, Jules. I'm outside, sitting in my car, and I can see the smoke from the fireplace. I don't know what's troubling you, but whatever it is, we can work it out. But I can't do anything for you if you won't talk to me." He paused, giving the banker a chance to pick up the phone, but nothing happened. He began talking again. "I'm your lawyer, Jules. That means that whatever's happening, I'm on—"

"You're fired, Becker. Get out of my driveway."

The harsh words erupted from the cell phone's speaker, startling Ed Becker into silence for a moment. He quickly recovered. "What's going on, Jules? What's happened?"

"A lot's happened," Jules Hartwick replied. "But you know all about it, don't you, Ed? Well, guess what? I know all about it too now. I know what's going on at the Bank, and I know what Madeline's been up to. And I know all about you. So just get off my property before I call the police."

The cellular phone went dead, leaving Ed Becker staring at the Hartwicks' mansion in stunned disbelief.

Twenty minutes later, with Jules Hartwick still refusing to answer either the door or the telephone, he finally gave up and started back down to the village. Somewhere, he was sure, there had to be someone who knew what had upset Jules so badly.

Unless, as Melissa Holloway had suggested, he'd just plain gone crazy.

* * *

"Oliver?" Lois Martin asked. Ed Becker had left the offices of the *Blackstone Chronicle*, having found out nothing more about what might be bothering Jules Hartwick than he'd known when he'd arrived half an hour earlier. Oliver had been sitting silently, head in hands, ever since. "Oliver?" Lois repeated. "Are you all right?"

The *Chronicle*'s editor and publisher pressed his fingers against his temples in a vain effort to stem the rising tide of pain. The headache had begun ten minutes ago, and was now threatening to overwhelm him not only with throbbing pain but with nausea as well. He leaned back in his chair and closed his eyes. The fluorescent light in the office, though no brighter than usual, was suddenly blinding him. "Have you ever had a migraine headache?" he asked.

"A long time ago," Lois replied, grimacing at the memory. "I had a few when I was in college. Worst thing I've ever been through." She lowered herself onto the chair that Ed Becker had vacated just minutes before, and regarded her boss worriedly. "You sure it's a migraine?"

"My head throbs, the lights are killing my eyes, and I'm starting to feel queasy. It's like someone's driving a spike right into the center of my head."

"Sounds like a migraine," Lois agreed. "When did it start?"

"This one? Maybe ten minutes ago. But this is maybe the third or fourth one I've had in the last month."

"Maybe you'd better go see Dr. Margolis."

"Or maybe Jules Hartwick ought to," Oliver countered. "Did you hear much of what Ed was saying?"

"I heard, but I can't believe it," Lois replied. "It just doesn't sound like Jules. I mean, the whole idea of Madeline Hartwick having an affair is ludicrous! And even if there's a major problem at the bank, Jules just isn't the type to go off the deep end."

"He's not the type to fire his lawyer over the phone either." Oliver sighed. "But he did it. What the hell is going on around here, Lois? Last month Elizabeth McGuire commits suicide, and now it sounds like Jules Hartwick is turning paranoid."

Lois Martin frowned. "You're not suggesting there's any connection between the two, are you?"

Before Oliver could reply, another stab of pain slashed through his head. He felt his skin turn cold and clammy, and his stomach began to churn. "Is there anything going on you can't handle?" he asked weakly when the wave of agony had receded to the point where he trusted himself to speak.

"There hasn't been anything going on that I couldn't handle for the last five years," Lois told him. "Go see the doctor, Oliver. Or at least go home, close the curtains, and lie down for a while." Oliver managed a nod and got shakily to his feet. "Can you drive?" Lois asked anxiously as Oliver used the desk to brace himself against the dizzy spell that struck him as he stood fully upright. "Maybe I better lock the office up for a few minutes and—"

"I'll be all right," Oliver assured her as the dizziness passed. He took a couple of experimental steps toward the front door, then managed a weak smile. "See? Perfectly steady."

"Just be careful," Lois cautioned as she helped him pull on his coat. "And call me when you get home. Otherwise, I'll come up to your house and fuss over you like an old hen. You'll hate it."

"I'll call," Oliver promised.

Getting into his Volvo, he winced as the engine caught and surged into noisy life, but a moment later, as the motor settled down to its normal rough idle, the throbbing pain in his head eased slightly. Pulling out of the parking space in front of the *Chronicle* office, he drove down Prospect to Amherst and started up the long slope of North Hill. Though the road was slick with packed snow, the Volvo threatened to go into a skid only once, and less than five minutes later Oliver pulled through the gates of the old Asylum and turned left, onto the side road that led to his cottage.

He pressed the remote control as he approached, and the door to his garage drew fully open just as he pulled into it. Getting out of the car, he opened the door that led directly into the laundry room of his house, but as he reached for the wall button that would close the garage door, he caught sight of the Asylum itself, looming on the crest of the hill half a hundred yards away at the top of the wide, curving drive.

Something about it seemed somehow different.

Abandoning the garage, Oliver stepped out into the bright, late morning sunlight and gazed up at the old building.

Its steeply pitched copper roof was covered with a thick blanket of glistening white snow. For a fleeting second he was almost able to imagine the building as it must have been a century ago, when it had first been built as a private home. He tried to envision it at Christmastime, when brightly colored sleighs drawn by horses laden with silver bells would have come up the hill bearing women in furs and hugely bustled dresses, and men in top hats and morning coats, to call on Jonas Connally, who had originally built the structure as a mansion for his family.

It hadn't lasted long. The patriarch of the Connally clan had died only a dozen years after his mansion was completed, and five years after that it had been converted to the only other use it had ever known.

A shelter for the insane.

Or had it actually been little more than a prison?

Oliver had never been sure, though over the years he'd

certainly heard plenty of stories from people who may or may not have known what they were talking about.

All he truly knew was that the imposing stone structure had always terrified him. Terrified him to the point where he'd been utterly unable to bring himself even to enter it. Yet this morning, with his head throbbing and his stomach churning, he found himself being drawn toward the long-abandoned building.

The cold of the morning forgotten, Oliver made his way through deep drifts and up the curving driveway toward the great oaken doors. A silence seemed to have fallen over North Hill, broken only by the sound of snow crunching beneath his feet.

Coming to the steps, he hesitated for a moment, then climbed up to the broad porch. He gazed for a moment at the huge wooden panels before reaching out to the great bronze lever that would release the latch.

As Oliver's fingers touched the ice cold metal, another wave of nausea seized him, and his hand jerked reflexively away as if the hardware had been red hot. His gorge rising, Oliver turned away once more and lurched back down the steps.

Falling to his knees, he retched into the snow, then, gasping for breath, got back to his feet and stumbled down the hill to his house. Unwilling to stay outside even long enough to unlock his front door, he went through the garage and into the laundry room, slamming the door behind him.

His heart pounding, Oliver leaned against the washing machine and tried to catch his breath. Slowly, the nausea in his belly eased and his breathing returned to normal, and even the stabbing pain in his head began to recede. When the telephone rang, he was able to make his way into the kitchen and pick up the extension with trembling fingers.

"Oliver?" Lois Martin said. "Is that you?"

"I-it's me," Oliver managed.

"Thank God," Lois breathed. "This is the third time I've called. If you hadn't answered, I was going to come up there. Are you all right?"

"I'm fine," Oliver said, though even as he uttered the words, he knew they were a lie.

Chapter 5

Madeline Hartwick turned off the interstate and slowed her Cadillac to precisely seven miles an hour above the posted speed limit. Another twenty minutes and they would be safely back in Blackstone, despite Celeste's insistence this morning that driving down to Boston today was insane. Madeline had been determined; they were both far too upset to sit at home all day, worrying over Jules's unprovoked outburst, and waiting tensely for him to return home from the bank.

"We'll go down to Boston, do some shopping, and have a nice lunch," she'd informed Celeste no more than ten minutes after Jules had left the house. Celeste had objected, but Madeline prevailed, and by the time they began browsing the shops on Newbury Street, Madeline had already convinced herself that Jules's crazy accusations had undoubtedly been brought on by the pressure he was under from the audit at the bank; when he got home, it would all have been forgotten. Nor had she killed anyone with the Cadillac as Celeste had so uncharitably insisted she was bound to do, given last night's snowstorm.

Shifting in the seat to ease the tension that always built up in her when she drove on the interstate, Madeline breathed a sigh of contentment. "I don't know about you," she said, glancing at her daughter, "but I feel a lot better."

Celeste—not nearly as sanguine about her father as her mother obviously was—rolled her eyes. "I'm not sure why bankrupting Daddy makes you feel better," she said. "And I certainly don't see how it makes up for the awful things he said this morning."

"It's really very simple, dear," her mother explained. "I vented my anger with my credit cards. Your father has atoned for what he said by buying me a perfectly lovely Valentino coat."

"But he doesn't know he bought it!" Celeste protested.

"He will when he gets the bill," Madeline reminded her. "And by then he'll feel so guilty about what he said that he won't even blink at how much it cost."

"But to have implied that you were having an affair—"

"Oh, pooh!" Madeline removed a hand from the steering wheel just long enough to brush her daughter's words dismissively away. "When you think about it, it's rather a compliment that he still thinks I'm attractive enough that someone would want to have an affair with me. Especially someone as young and handsome as Andrew!"

"Mother!"

"Oh, for heaven's sake, Celeste—don't be such a prude. By the time you and Andrew have been married as long as your father and I, you'll understand that things are not always easy. If you don't, you'll already be divorced several times by the time you're my age. There are lots of rough patches in any marriage, dear. You have to learn to deal with them without cutting and running."

"But what Daddy said was unforgivable—" Celeste began.

But Madeline, having heard it all three times already today, didn't let her finish. "Everything is forgivable, if you wish to forgive," she cut in. "And I don't wish to discuss it any further. Let's just go home and see how your father is when he comes home from the bank today. All right?"

The sigh Celeste uttered was far more out of resignation than from contentment, but she decided to let the argument go, at least for now. If her mother was determined not to see that something had gone seriously wrong with her father, there would be no talking her out of it. At least not right now. Lapsing into silence, she contented herself with gazing at the wintery scene outside the car. Maybe this weekend she and Andrew would drive over to Stowe and do some skiing. Assuming, of course, that she and Andrew were still together by the end of the week. If her father started spreading his horrible story around the bank, there was no telling what Andrew might do. But maybe her mother was right, and by now the whole terrible incident was over with.

A few minutes later, though, as they pulled into the driveway, Celeste saw the smoke curling up from the den's chimney and glanced at the clock on the Cadillac's dashboard. Just a little after four. What was her father doing at home? He never came home before six.

As the Cadillac pulled up under the porte cochere, Celeste saw the tracks in the snow that still marked the path Ed Becker had taken that morning. "Something's wrong, Mother," she said. She got out of the car, but instead of going to the trunk to help Madeline carry the packages in, she walked farther up the driveway until she could clearly see the path someone had beaten into the snow. "Mother, it looks like someone was trying to get into the house," she called out.

"Well, I'm sure there's a reasonable explanation for it," Madeline said a moment later as she stood next to her daughter, her arms laden with packages. "Perhaps your father—"

"Why would Daddy be trying to break into his own house?" Celeste asked. "Maybe we shouldn't even go in! Maybe we should call the police—"

"Nonsense!" Madeline declared. "For heaven's sake, child, we'd look like perfect fools. Besides, you yourself just pointed out the smoke coming from the fireplace in your father's den. Unless the world has changed a great deal more than I think it has, burglars do not build fires to keep them warm while they riffle your house! Bring the rest of the packages in from the car while I go see what's been going on here."

Ignoring Celeste's protests, Madeline mounted the steps to the porch, then fumbled with her keys until she found the right one. "Jules?" she called out as she set her packages down on the table in the entry hall. "Jules, are you here?" When there was no answer, she crossed the foyer to the library and rapped sharply on the closed door to her husband's den. "Jules? May I come in?" There was no answer. "Jules!"

A muffled voice came from the other side of the door. "Go away."

Madeline's hand closed on the doorknob and she tried to turn it.

Locked.

"Jules, I want to talk to you!"

When there was no response from inside the den, Madeline mounted the stairs, heading for her dressing room. She kept a spare set of keys to every door in the huge old house in the top drawer of her vanity. But when she came to her dressing room she stopped abruptly. The door was ajar. Beyond it, every drawer and every closet door stood open, and her lingerie had been scattered across the carpeted floor. The anger she'd so deliberately dissipated in the shops along Newbury Street came flooding back. Jules never came into her dressing room, just as she never went into his den. Today, though, he'd not only entered her sanctuary, but searched through her things! Surely he hadn't actually expected to find proof of the affair he imagined she was having! It was ludicrous! Intolerable!

Ignoring the tangle of clothes on the floor, Madeline went to her vanity. Though it was clear that every drawer had been gone through, everything still seemed to be there, and she quickly found the ring of keys.

Celeste was just coming into the foyer when she got back to the foot of the stairs. Together the two women returned to the locked door to the den. Madeline once again knocked loudly on the mahogany panels, and when there was no reply, she began trying the keys on the ring until one fit. She heard the bolt click back and turned the knob once more. The door swung open.

Jules glowered at her from behind his desk. A nearly empty bottle of scotch sat at his elbow.

She crossed to the desk. "I don't know what's wrong, Jules," she said softly. "But I do know that finishing that bottle won't help."

"You know what's wrong, you tramp!"

As if acting under its own volition, Madeline's hand flashed out and slapped her husband across the face, but even before the sting on her palm had died away, she regretted her action. "Oh, God, Jules, I'm sorry. I didn't mean—"

"You've been wanting to do that for years, haven't you?" Jules growled, his words slurring. "Do you think I haven't known? Well, I know, Madeline. I know everything."

Madeline bit her lower lip to keep her temper in check, then took a deep breath. "All right," she said. "I can see there's no point in talking to you right now. Dinner will be ready at seven. Come to the table or not, as you see fit." Picking up the bottle of scotch and taking it with her, Madeline left the study, pulling the door closed behind her.

"What is it?" Celeste asked. "Mother, what's wrong with him?"

"I don't know," Madeline replied. "But I think it's time to call Dr. Margolis."

The two women went back through the library to the foyer, where a telephone sat on a table near the base of the wide staircase. Picking up the receiver, Madeline dialed Philip Margolis's office. His nurse answered on the second ring.

"Nancy?" Madeline said. "It's Madeline Hartwick. I would like to speak to Philip, please."

"I'm afraid he's in Concord, Mrs. Hartwick," Nancy Conway told her. "Is there something I can do for you?"

Madeline hesitated. Though she'd known Nancy Conway for twenty years, and liked her, she was well aware that Nancy had never kept a secret in her life, and never passed on a story without embellishing it. If she even hinted at the things Jules was doing and saying, by tomorrow morning everyone in Blackstone would have heard that he'd lost his mind. Better to deal with Jules herself tonight, she decided, and talk directly to Philip Margolis in the morning. "I don't think so, Nancy," she said. "It's nothing that can't wait."

Chapter 6

As the symphony of chimes signifying the dinner hour echoed through the Hartwicks' vast house, Madeline carried the last plate into the breakfast room, where she, Jules, and Celeste invariably ate when they were alone. Tonight, in a special effort to please her troubled husband, Madeline had covered the table with one of her best lace cloths, set out the sterling candelabra that had belonged to Jules's mother—the same candelabra that could be seen in the portrait of her that they'd found in the attic, and which now hung in the library—and gotten out the Limoges china with the hunting pattern that had always been his favorite. Celeste had even found a dozen roses at the florist that perfectly matched the red of the burgundy Madeline had opened half an hour ago.

Madeline turned the outside lights on, transforming the dark landscape beyond the windows into a brilliantly sparkling winterscape. As she waited for her husband and daughter to join her, she decided that no matter how bad Jules's mood had been today, the dinner she'd prepared, and the setting she created in which to serve it, couldn't possibly fail to cheer him up. But when Celeste came into the room as the last of the clocks' chimes died away, her father was not with her.

"Do you think he'll come at all?" Celeste asked as she took her seat while her mother poured the wine.

"I don't know," Madeline replied, sounding far more calm than she felt.

"But—"

"But nothing," Madeline cut in, perfectly matching the level of wine in the third Waterford goblet to that in the other two. "If he won't tell us what's wrong . . ." Her voice died away as she heard Jules's footsteps coming through the dining room.

When he appeared in the doorway, she forced a smile that managed to mask the many emotions that had been churning through her all day. "I've fixed all your favorites," she said, moving toward Jules to take his arm and draw him into the room. When he pulled away from her, she chose to ignore it, and pulled his chair out for him. "Filet mignon, just on the medium side of medium rare, a baked potato with all the things that are bad for you, green beans with almonds, and a Caesar salad. And I broke out a Pauillac, one of the 'eighty-fives."

Jules eyed the table carefully, as if searching for something that might be ready to strike out at him, and for a moment Madeline was afraid he was going to bolt from the room. But then he moved away from his chair and seated himself in her own. He looked up at her, his eyes glinting in the candlelight. "Suppose I sit in your chair tonight?" he asked, a strange smile twisting his lips—one that seemed to Madeline to be oddly triumphant, as if he'd just won some kind of victory over her. "Would that be all right with you?"

"Of course," she replied, immediately settling herself into what was ordinarily Jules's place at the table. It felt distinctly odd, but if this was what it would take to soothe her husband, so be it. She picked up her knife and fork, cut off a small portion of the steak, and put it in her mouth.

Jules abruptly stood up. "I've changed my mind. I'll sit there after all."

Her jaw tightening, but saying nothing, Madeline stood and picked up the plate in front of her.

"Leave it there," Jules commanded.

Celeste, who until now had said nothing at all, finally broke her silence. "For heaven's sake, Daddy, what are you doing? Did you think Mother poisoned your food or something? It's as if . . ." Celeste's words died away as her father's eyes bored into her, glowing with a feverish light she'd never seen in them before. She quickly shifted her own gaze to her mother, who shook her head just enough for Celeste to understand that she would do well to change the subject. "Maybe we could talk about the wedding," she began, realizing the moment the words were out of her mouth that she'd made a mistake.

"And what wedding would that be?" her father demanded, his voice ice cold.

"M-mine and Andrew's," Celeste stammered, her words barely audible.

Jules's gaze pierced her. "Really, Celeste, how stupid do you think I am?" Once again Celeste glanced at her mother, but this time her father saw the movement of her eyes. "Don't look at her, Celeste. She can't help you this time. I'm on to her, and I'm on to Andrew. I'm even on to you."

Celeste set down her fork. She had begun to tremble. "Why are you doing this, Daddy? Why are you talking like everyone's out to get you? Why are—"

"Aren't they?" Jules suddenly bellowed, slamming his fist down on the table so hard his wineglass fell over. A dark stain spread like blood from a wound. "There won't be a wedding, Celeste! Not to that bastard Andrew Sterling, anyway. And as of tomorrow morning, he'll be out of the Bank. Do you understand? How dare he think he can take over my own Bank! And how dare you even think of marrying him! Don't you understand? He wants everything I have. My Bank, my wife, my daughter—

everything! Well, he won't get it! None of it! None of it, goddamn it!"

Bursting into tears, Celeste fled from the table. Madeline rose as if to follow her daughter, but as she heard Celeste's feet pounding up the stairs, she turned back to face her husband, her own eyes now almost as angry as his. "Have you gone out of your mind, Jules?" she demanded. "I called Dr. Margolis earlier, and I'm going to call him again in the morning. In the meantime, I suggest—"

"You'll suggest nothing!" Jules stood, plunging his right hand deep into the pocket of his pants. "What are you planning to do, put me in the Asylum? Well, you won't get away with it, Madeline! When I tell people what you've been up to—you and Andrew, and Celeste too—you'll all be in jail! Or have you got everyone else in the plot too?" His eyes narrowed to tiny, suspicious slits. "You'd better tell me what you're planning, Madeline. I'll find out, you know. One way or another, I'll find out everything."

He edged toward her, but Madeline turned and strode from the breakfast room. By the time he'd moved through the dining room and the small parlor, she had reached the foot of the broad staircase.

"I'm going upstairs, Jules," she told him, her eyes fixed steadily on him, her voice calm. "I'm not having an affair with anyone, and I'm not out to ruin your life, and neither are Celeste and Andrew. We all love you, and we all want to help you." She paused, then spoke again, using the soothing tones that had always calmed Celeste when she was a child. "It's going to be all right, Jules. Whatever is wrong, I'm going to fix. Right now, I'm going to go up and take care of our daughter. Then, in a few minutes, I'll be back downstairs, and you and I can figure it all out." When he made no reply, she turned and hurried up the stairs.

Jules, clutching the locket tightly in his right hand,

watched her disappear onto the second floor. Take care of Celeste, indeed! He could almost hear them, whispering together in Celeste's room, scheming against him.

Scheming what?

Would Madeline really call Margolis and have him locked away in the Asylum?

Of course she would! She'd do anything to get rid of him, so she and Andrew could take over the Bank.

And Celeste was part of it too, of course!

How stupid he'd been not to have seen it coming months ago! But of course that had been the genius of their plot—Celeste would pretend to be in love with Andrew so he'd never suspect what Andrew and Madeline were up to! But he'd figured it out in time.

And he'd stop it too.

He was at the foot of the stairs; suddenly, one of the lights on the telephone went on.

They were trying to call someone! One of their co-conspirators, no doubt!

He started up the stairs, intent on stopping them, then realized they'd have locked Celeste's door against him.

The phones!

He could tear out the phones!

Instead of going up, he dashed back through the dining room and into the kitchen, then down the back stairs to the basement. Groping in the dark, he found the light switch. The bright glare of a naked bulb pierced the darkness around him.

The laundry room.

That's where the main electrical box was, and he was almost sure that's where they'd put the box for the new phone system he'd had installed last year.

He darted into the laundry room, felt for the light switch, and a moment later found the telephone's control box right where he remembered it.

Dozens of wires sprouted from the connector boards that were mounted on the wall next to the controller, and

Jules, after staring at them for a split second, began indiscriminately jerking them loose.

Through nothing more then pure chance, the very first wires he tore free from the boards were the lines coming in from the outside. Though he kept tearing at the wires, the phones throughout the house had already gone dead.

Chapter 7

*T*he last wire jerked free from the panel next to the control unit. Jules Hartwick stepped back, breathing hard, staring at his handiwork, listening to the silence that had descended on the house.

What had they thought he'd do? How big a fool did they take him for? Even as he sat in his den all day, he'd been able to hear them. Hear them as clearly in his own mind as if they'd been in the room with him.

Talking about him.

Laughing at him.

Plotting against him.

But he'd outsmarted them. Now he was in control, and they had no one to talk to but each other.

Who had they been calling?

The traitor, Andrew Sterling?

The quack, Philip Margolis?

Or someone else?

There were so many of them out there.

Enemies.

They weren't just in his home and in his Bank.

They were all over town. Watching him. Whispering about him.

And plotting. Always plotting.

How long had it been going on? How long had they all been able to fool him, making him think they were his friends? Well, it was all over now. Everything was crystal clear, and finally he was in control of his own life again. And it would stay that way.

Jules left the laundry room, careful not to turn off the lights, not to offer his enemies any darkness in which to hide. He moved through the basement, turning on every light until the warren of dusty rooms beneath the house was free from any shadows in which his enemies might lurk. Then, satisfied that no lights remained unlit, he went back up to the kitchen. There, too, he turned on every light, filling the room with a brilliant glow.

From the huge rack above the carving counter, he chose a knife with a ten-inch blade, honed to razor sharpness by years of perfect care. Its smooth haft, carved from ebony nearly a century earlier, fit perfectly in his hand, and as his fingers tightened on it he felt the strength of the hardwood seep from the weapon into his body. Fingering it now as he'd fingered the locket a few minutes earlier, he left the kitchen and moved through the butler's pantry and into the dining room, still turning on every light he found, washing the house free of any dark corners in which his enemies might conceal themselves.

Moving as silently as a wraith, Jules Hartwick prowled the main floor of his house, banishing the darkness from its rooms as the locket he carried with him had banished reason from his mind.

Madeline and Celeste listened to the silence of the house.

When the phone had suddenly gone dead in Madeline's hand while she was waiting for Philip Margolis's answering service to come back on the line, she'd assumed that the connection had merely been lost by the service itself. But when she pressed the redial button and nothing happened, her impatience with the incompetence of the answering service gave way to fear. Surely she was wrong!

Jules was upset, but he wouldn't cut the phone lines—would he?

She stabbed at the buttons that should have connected to one of the other lines that came into the house. None of the lights came on. There was a deadness to the silence in the receiver that told her the phones were no longer working at all. She slammed the handset back onto its cradle. Her thoughts darted first one way then another, like mice in a maze.

Raise the window and call for help?

She cringed at the mere thought of the kind of talk that would cause. If the problems at the bank were bad now, they'd be ten times worse by tomorrow, when everyone in town would know that Jules had gone—

She cut herself off, refusing to use the word "insane" even in the privacy of her own mind. Jules was under a strain—a severe strain—but he was *not* insane! Therefore, whatever had upset him could be dealt with. *She* could deal with it. Taking a deep breath to steady her nerves, she turned to Celeste. "Stay here," she instructed her daughter. "I'm going downstairs to talk to your father."

"Are you crazy?" Celeste asked. "Mother, he's cut off the phones! You don't know what he'll do next."

Madeline steeled herself against the fear that was creeping through her, knowing that if she gave in to it even for a moment she would lose her courage entirely. "Your father won't hurt me," she said. "We've been married for twenty-five years, and there's never been a hint of violence in him. I don't think he's going to start now." She started toward the door.

"I'm coming with you," Celeste told her.

Madeline was tempted to argue, but as she remembered the look she'd seen in Jules's eyes as he glared at her from the foot of the stairs, she changed her mind. Opening the door to Celeste's bedroom, she stepped out into the hall.

The house was as silent as a tomb.

Unconsciously taking her daughter's hand in her own, Madeline moved to the head of the stairs. She was just about to peer over the banister to the entry hall below when the silence was shattered by the gong of the grandfather clock striking the half hour. As both Madeline and Celeste jumped at the noise, all the other clocks in the house began sounding as well, the rooms resonating with a cacophony of chimes and bells.

Then, as quickly as it had begun, it was over, and once more a shroud of silence dropped over them.

"Where is he?" Celeste whispered. "What's he doing?"

Before Madeline could answer, Jules appeared at the bottom of the stairs. His hands behind his back, he glowered up at them.

"Stay here," Madeline instructed Celeste firmly. "I'm going to try to talk to him. If anything happens, lock yourself in your room. You'll be safe in there."

"Mother, don't," Celeste pleaded, but Madeline was already starting slowly down the long flight of stairs, her eyes fixed on her husband.

Do not be afraid of him, she told herself. He won't hurt you.

From her room in the house next door, Rebecca Morrison watched curiously as every window on the main floor of the Hartwicks' house blossomed into light.

Were the Hartwicks going to have another party?

Surely not—no catering truck had arrived, nor had she seen any of the waiters Madeline always hired when she was having a big party. And it was already seven-thirty, long after the time the parties next door invariably began.

Yet she was certain that something unusual was happening, for except when the Hartwicks were having a party, the lights in the rooms they weren't using were never left burning, any more than they were in her own house.

"Rebecca? What are you doing, child?"

Rebecca jumped at her aunt's words and instantly dropped the curtain she'd been peeping through. As she turned to face her aunt, Martha Ward's eyes narrowed and her lips pursed in disapproval.

"Are you spying on the neighbors again, Rebecca?" Martha demanded.

"I was just looking," Rebecca said. "And the oddest thing is happening, Aunt Martha. All the—"

"I do not wish to hear," Martha interjected, her own words neatly cutting her niece's short. "Nor do you need to watch. We shall go to the chapel and pray for your forgiveness."

"But Aunt Martha," Rebecca began again, "I think maybe—"

"Silence!" Martha Ward commanded. "I shall not be tainted with your sins, Rebecca. Come with me."

Rebecca, with one last glance toward the curtained windows that looked out at the house next door, silently, obediently, followed her aunt to the chapel. As the Gregorian chants began to play, she knelt before the altar and the glowing candles whose heat and smoke seemed to draw the very air from the room. Her aunt began mumbling the prayers, and Rebecca tried to close her mind to whatever might be happening next door.

It's none of my business, she told herself. I must remember that it is none of my business.

Madeline Hartwick came to the bottom of the stairs. Her husband's eyes were still fixed on her, and in the brilliant light of the chandelier suspended from the ceiling of the great entry hall, she could see clearly the hatred emanating from them.

"Go back to your room, Celeste," she said, once again steeling herself to betray none of the fear that was suddenly coursing through her. Whatever had happened to Jules—whatever madness had seized him—had worsened in just the few minutes she'd been away from him, and though she refused to betray her terror to him or to their daughter, she had to protect Celeste. "Lock your door. You'll be safe there."

For the smallest instant she was afraid Celeste was going to ignore her words, and when she saw Jules's gaze flicker toward the stairs, she uttered a silent prayer.

Leave her alone! If your madness demands a victim, take me!

As if he'd heard her unspoken words, Jules's eyes fixed once more on her. In the silence that followed, she heard Celeste's door thud shut and, a second later, the hard click of the lock snapping into place. "What is it, Jules?" she asked softly. "What is it you want of me?"

Without warning, Jules's left arm snaked out, spun her around, and clamped her against his chest. At the same instant, she saw the blade of the knife glimmering in the light of the chandelier, then felt cold steel caress her neck with a touch as light as a feather.

A deadly feather.

She froze, her nostrils flaring, every muscle in her body going rigid.

Then she felt Jules's hot breath on her neck and smelled the whiskey he'd been drinking all through the day.

"I could kill you," he whispered. "All I have to do is pull the knife across your throat. It would be easy, Madeline. And you deserve it, don't you?"

When she made no reply, his grip on her tightened, and she felt the blade of the knife etch her skin. Her mind raced and she began speaking, the words boiling up out of some well of defense she hadn't known she possessed. "Yes," she heard herself saying. "I didn't think you'd find out. I didn't think you were smart enough. But I was wrong, Jules. I should have known I couldn't fool you. I should have known you'd find out. And I'm sorry, Jules. I'm so very, very sorry."

She began crying then, and let herself go limp in his violent embrace. Once again his grip on her tightened. He steered her across the entry hall, then through the parlor, the dining room, and the kitchen. Then they were at the top of the stairs leading to the basement. Madeline gazed down the steep flight at the concrete floor below.

"Lies!" she heard Jules whisper harshly in her ear. "All of it has been nothing but lies, without so much as a teaspoon of truth!" He released her, the knife dropping away from her throat as he hurled her away from him. Madeline reached out frantically, groping for the wall, the banister, anything that might stop her as she pitched forward.

There was nothing.

As she plunged headfirst down the stairs, the fear that had been rising within her broke through the dam of self-control she had struggled to hold intact. A scream of terror erupted from her throat, shattering the silence in the house, only to be cut off a second later as her head struck the concrete floor.

As Madeline's body lay broken at the foot of the stairs, Jules—his right hand still clutching the knife—slowly descended to the basement.

In the Hartwick mansion at the top of Harvard Street, all that could be heard was an eerie quiet.

A silence as deep as the grave.

Chapter 8

*A*ndrew Sterling punched Celeste Hartwick's number into the keypad of his portable phone for the third time, and listened with growing worry to the continuous ringing at the other end of the line. The line had been busy when he'd first dialed her number fifteen minutes ago, but when he'd tried again, he'd gotten no answer. It made no sense: he was sure Celeste had been planning to have dinner with her parents tonight. Why was no one answering the phone? The memory of Jules's strange behavior at the bank that morning only increased Andrew's mounting uneasiness. Following the tenth unanswered ring on Celeste's line, he hung up and dialed the operator. After waiting thirty seconds he heard a laconic voice inform him that "that line is currently out of order, sir. Would you like me to connect you with repair service?" Unwilling to get involved in what he suspected would turn into an impenetrable bureaucratic maze, Andrew hung up.

He pulled a parka on over the flannel shirt into which he'd changed after leaving the office an hour ago, and, gulping down the last bite of the microwaved pizza that had served as dinner, he went out to his five-year-old Ford Escort—all his bank salary could support in the way of a car—and prayed there was enough tread left on the tires to let him get up Harvard Street to the Hartwicks' house.

A few flakes of snow drifted down as the Escort's

engine coughed into reluctant life. By the time Andrew pulled away from the curb, a sharp wind had come up. The light dusting of a minute or two earlier was rapidly developing into a heavy snowfall. He'd gone only a block when the night filled with a swirling white cloud that cut visibility down to a few yards. As the wiper struggled to keep the windshield clear, Andrew crept toward North Hill, praying that the Escort would find the power to make it up the snow-slicked grade of Harvard Street.

It seemed to Celeste as if hours had passed since she'd heard her mother's muffled scream, cut off almost the instant it had begun.

Oh God! Had her father hurt her mother?

Maybe even killed her?

But that couldn't be possible—could it? Her parents adored one another! But as she stood rooted to the floor behind the locked door to her room, images of her father flashed through her mind.

This morning at the breakfast table, his eyes burning with jealousy as he hurled insane accusations at her mother . . .

This afternoon when they'd come home and found him drinking in his den . . .

A few minutes ago at the dinner table, accusing not only her mother, but herself as well . . .

Insane! It was all insane!

He was insane!

Rattling the doorknob to be certain the lock was secure, she went to the window and peered out into the night. Snow was falling rapidly now, and though she could still make out Martha Ward's house next door, and even the VanDeventers' across the street, no lights showed. But maybe if she yelled, someone would hear her. She struggled with the window, finally managed to lift it, then began wrestling with the storm window outside. But what was the use? Every house on the street had storm windows, and even if she succeeded in opening hers, her voice would be all but lost in the snowstorm.

Out!

She had to get out! If she could just get to the garage and her car—

Her heart sank as she remembered that her mother's car was still sitting in the porte cochere. Even if the snow hadn't made the driveway impassable, her mother's car did. But she could still get to a neighbor's—*someone* had to be home; if not the VanDeventers, then in the house next door. Martha Ward never went anywhere except to church, and Rebecca went only to the library.

She went back to the door and pressed her ear against it, listening.

Silence.

Her fingers trembling, she twisted the key in the lock. When the bolt clicked back, it seemed unnaturally loud.

Again she listened, but still the house was silent.

Finally she risked opening the door a crack and peered out into the wide corridor.

Empty.

She stepped out of her room and started toward the top of the stairs, then heard a door close downstairs. Celeste stopped dead in her tracks, close enough to the head of the stairs that she could gaze down into the entry hall below.

Her father appeared from the dining room. Even from where she stood, Celeste could hear him muttering to himself. His clothes were smeared with blood. When he abruptly stopped and looked up as if sensing her presence, his eyes seemed to have glazed over.

"Whore!" he said, his voice rasping as he spat the word at her. "Did you think I'd never figure it out?"

He was at the foot of the stairs now. Celeste gasped as

she saw him lunge forward, taking the steps two at a time. Panic galvanizing her into action, Celeste fled back into her room, slamming the door and throwing the lock, then collapsing against the thick mahogany panel, her heart pounding.

Only as she heard her father grasp the knob and rattle the door did she realize her mistake. Instead of retreating back to her room, she should have fled past it to the back stairs. By now she'd be out of the house and into the street.

She'd be safe.

Instead she was trapped in her room like a rat in a cage.

How could she have been so stupid?

Her father stopped rattling the doorknob, and once again silence fell over the house. Celeste remained where she was, her heart pounding. Was he still out there? She didn't know. The seconds dragged on, turning into minutes. Should she risk unlocking the door and peeking out? But then, even as she reached for the knob, she froze. She could feel him on the other side of the door, feel his insane rage as palpably as if it were seeping through the wood to engulf her.

"Daddy?" she whimpered. "Daddy, please. Tell me what's wrong. Tell me what's happened to you. I love you, Daddy. I love—"

Her words were cut off by something—something hard and heavy—striking the door. The force of the blow, transmitted directly through the wood, was sharp enough to startle her into jumping back from the door, and as she stood staring at it, trying to fathom what was happening on the other side, she heard the sound again.

Pounding!

He was pounding with a hammer!

Trying to break the door down?

The pounding stopped for a moment, then began again,

and suddenly Celeste realized that he wasn't trying to break the door down at all!

He was nailing it shut.

A wave of hopelessness overwhelmed her. The phones were gone, the snow was too heavy and the neighbors too far away for anyone to hear her calling for help.

Stupid! How could she have been so stupid?

Andrew Sterling automatically steered into the skid as the Escort slewed to the left, threatened to spin around and slam into a parked car, then found its traction again. Making no further attempt to keep the car on the right side of Harvard Street, he nosed it slowly up the hill. The snow, packing under the pressure of the tires into a slick glaze of ice, kept threatening his control of the vehicle. By the time he could finally make out the gate to the Hartwicks' mansion, his body was knotted with tension and his hands ached from gripping the steering wheel too hard. But at last he was able to turn the car into the driveway. Leaving it close to the gate, he got out and started toward the house, which was blazing with light. Even as he watched, more lights came on on the second floor, but when he mounted the steps to the front porch and rang the bell, there was no response.

But someone was home.

Madeline's Cadillac was under the porte cochere, and someone had been turning the lights on upstairs.

He rang the bell again, waited a few more seconds, then tried the knob. The door was locked.

Pulling the hood of his parka up, Andrew tramped up the driveway, slogging through the drifting snow, which by morning would block it completely. Banging as hard as he could on the kitchen door, he called out, but his words sounded muffled even to himself, and he was sure they would be utterly inaudible to anyone inside the house. He started to turn away in order to go back to the front door, then changed his mind.

Someone was inside, but no one was answering the door.

The phones weren't working.

And something had been wrong with Jules Hartwick this morning.

Making up his mind, Andrew Sterling stepped back, lowered his left shoulder, and hurled himself against the kitchen door. Though the door held, he heard the distinct sound of wood cracking. On the second try the frame gave way and the door flew open as the striker plate clattered to the floor.

Andrew Sterling stepped into the kitchen.

For a moment everything appeared normal. Then he saw them.

Spots on the floor.

Bright red spots.

Blood red.

His pulse quickening, Andrew followed the trail of blood through the butler's pantry, the dining room, the parlor, and into the entry hall.

The trail stopped at the bottom of the stairs.

Andrew paused. Though the house was silent, he felt danger all around him.

Danger, and fear.

"Celeste?" he called. "Celeste!"

"Andrew?" Her voice was muffled, coming from somewhere on the second floor. Racing up the stairs, Andrew called out to her again as he reached the second-floor landing. His words died on his lips when he saw the door to her room.

Nails—three of them—had been clumsily pounded into the wood at a steep enough angle to pin the door to its frame. Andrew rattled the knob, then spoke again. "Celeste? Are you all right?"

"It's D-Daddy!" Celeste replied, her voice catching.

"He's—oh, God, Andrew, he's gone crazy! He's done something to Mother—"

"Unlock the door," Andrew told her.

As soon as he heard the click of the lock, he hurled his weight against the door, but the thick mahogany frame was stronger than the frame of the kitchen door had been. By the time the wood finally split away and allowed the door to open, his shoulder was aching and he was panting.

"Where's your mother?" he said, ignoring the stab of pain that shot through his shoulder as she pressed herself against him, sobbing.

"I don't know—downstairs, I think. They were at the foot of the stairs, and he—he had a knife, and—"

Andrew suppressed a groan. He'd followed the trail of blood the wrong way. Jules must have taken Madeline down to the basement. "Where is he now?" Andrew asked, his voice urgent.

"I—I don't know," Celeste stammered. "He nailed my door shut, then he—oh, God, Andrew, I just don't know!"

Suddenly Andrew remembered. The lights. It had to have been Jules turning on the lights. If he was still up here—

Both of them froze as they heard footsteps.

Footsteps from above. "He's on the third floor," Celeste whispered. "What are we going to do? Did he take Mother up there?"

"The basement," Andrew told her. "Come on. We've got to find her and get out of here!"

Half pulling and half supporting Celeste, Andrew led her downstairs, then into the kitchen. When they were at the door to the basement, he held her by the shoulders and looked directly into her eyes. "I'm going to go down and see if I can find your mother. If you hear your father coming down, go outside." Fishing in his pocket, he found his car keys. "My car's in the driveway. I'll try to catch up with you, but if I can't, take the car and get away."

Celeste shook her head. "No. I won't leave you and Mother with him."

Andrew started to argue with her, then changed his mind, knowing it would be useless. "I'll get back as soon as I can." Leaving her standing in the kitchen, he raced down the stairs.

He found Madeline in the laundry room. Her dress was soaked with blood, and she lay on the floor, her wrists and ankles bound with duct tape. Another piece sealed her mouth.

Her eyes were closed and she lay still, and for a moment Andrew was afraid she might be dead. But when he knelt down and pressed a finger against her bloody neck, he felt a pulse. Ripping the duct tape from her mouth, he lifted her in his arms and started up the stairs. A moment later he emerged into the kitchen. Celeste, her face ashen, lurched toward him.

"Mama?" she gasped, unconsciously using a word that hadn't crossed her lips since she was a child. Her eyes flicked to Andrew's. "Is she—" Her voice failed her and she left the question unspoken.

"She's alive," Andrew said. "We've got to get her to the hospital."

With Madeline in his arms, he followed Celeste through the dining room and parlor, and into the entry hall. Celeste was just opening the front door when there was a roar of rage from the stairs.

"Bastard!" Jules bellowed. "How dare you come here?" He was standing halfway up the stairs, the knife clutched in one hand, and what looked like some kind of necklace dangling from the other. His face was twitching, and his eyes, burning like coals, seemed to have sunk deep into his head.

For one brief instant Andrew was frozen in place, but then he met Jules Hartwick's insane gaze. "I'm taking them away from here, Mr. Hartwick," he said very quietly. "Don't try to stop me."

"Traitor," Jules Hartwick snarled. "Fornicator. Adulterer. I should kill all of you. And I could, Andrew. I could kill you as easily as I cut the whore's throat." He started down the stairs, moving slowly, his eyes never leaving Andrew.

Celeste, still at the door, stared in horror at her father. There was nothing left of the man she'd known only yesterday. The person who was advancing toward her now, spittle drooling from one corner of his mouth, his hair matted to his scalp, his eyes glittering insanely, bore no resemblance to her father at all. "Hurry, Andrew," she said. "Please."

Pulling the front door open, she stumbled out into the snow and ran for Andrew's car. Andrew, still carrying Madeline's unconscious body, strode out onto the porch, then turned back to look at Jules once again. He was at the foot of the stairs now, and starting toward the door.

Wordlessly, Andrew turned and hurried out into the night. By the time Andrew got to the car, Jules had emerged onto the porch. "Liars!" he shouted. "Prevaricators! I'll kill you all! I swear, I'll kill you all!"

As Andrew laid Madeline on the backseat, then slid into the front seat next to Celeste, Jules stumbled down the driveway toward them, bellowing curses, the butcher knife held high. Celeste put the car in gear and began backing out of the driveway. Jules lunged toward the car, but it was too late. He sprawled out onto the driveway, facedown, then pulled himself to his knees.

"Celeste, wait," Andrew said as Jules stared mindlessly into the glare of the headlights. "Maybe we'd better help him. Maybe—"

But Celeste kept her foot on the accelerator, backing the car out of the driveway, then slewing it around so it was pointed downhill. "No," she said as she started down the steep slope. "That's not Daddy. That's not anyone I know."

As he watched the car disappear into the snow, Jules Hartwick let out one more bellow of rage. The fingers of his left hand closed on the locket, and then, with a howl of frustration, he hurled it after the departing car.

And as the locket left his fingers, his mind cleared.

The paranoia that had robbed him of his sanity drained away as suddenly as it had come over him.

But the memories of what he'd done did not.

Every word he had uttered, every accusation he had made, echoed in his mind. But what horrified him most was an image.

An image of Madeline, crumpled at the bottom of the basement stairs, her neck bleeding, her body broken.

Sobbing, Jules Hartwick staggered to his feet. He lurched down the driveway, the hand that had held the locket only a moment ago now reaching out as if to call back the car that was carrying away everything he'd ever loved. He stood in the street, watching until it completely disappeared, then turned and began walking the other way.

A moment later he too disappeared into the snowy night.

Chapter 9

"*Liars! Prevaricators! I'll kill you all! I swear, I'll kill you all!*"

Although muffled by the closed and curtained windows of Martha Ward's chapel, the furious words still cut through the soft drone of Gregorian chants, startling Rebecca Morrison out of the reverie she'd fallen into as her aunt's prayers droned on. Her knees protesting painfully as she rose from the kneeling position her aunt always insisted upon, Rebecca moved to the window and pulled the curtain aside just far enough to get a glimpse of the house next door.

Every light had been turned on; even the tiny dormers in the roof glowed brightly through the falling snow. A car—Rebecca was almost certain it was Andrew Sterling's—was backing out of the driveway. For a moment Rebecca wasn't quite sure from where the shouted words had come, but then Jules Hartwick suddenly appeared in the glare of the car's headlights.

He was lurching down the driveway. Through the swirl of falling snow Rebecca could make out the contortions of his face.

And see the knife he held in his hand.

She watched, transfixed, as he stumbled toward the retreating car, then collapsed into the snow.

As he rose back up to his knees, howling like a wounded animal, then staggered away, Rebecca's mind raced.

81

What had happened next door?

Had Mr. Hartwick killed someone?

Who had been in the car?

Call someone.

She had to call someone.

Her fingers releasing the edge of the curtain, she backed away from the window, only to find herself facing her aunt.

Martha, eyes shining with the rapture of her prayers, was glaring furiously at her. "How dare you!" the older woman said in a furious whisper. "How could you commit the very sin for which you were praying for forgiveness! And in the chapel!"

"But something's wrong, Aunt Martha! Mr. Hartwick has a knife and—"

"Silence!" Martha commanded, holding her finger to her niece's lips. "I will not have the chapel vilified by your gossip! I will not have—"

But Rebecca heard no more. Brushing her aunt's hand away, she hurried out of the chapel and made her way to the front parlor on the other side of the foyer. Picking up the telephone, she was about to dial the emergency number when she hesitated.

What if she was wrong? Her mind echoed with everything she'd been told over the years, first by her aunt, then by librarian Germaine Wagner, then by almost everyone she knew:

"You don't understand, Rebecca."

"No one expects more of you than you can do, Rebecca."

"It's all right, Rebecca. Let someone else worry about it."

"Now, Rebecca, you know you don't always understand what's happening. . . ."

"Just do as you're told, Rebecca."

"You don't understand, Rebecca!"

But she knew what she'd seen! Mr. Hartwick had been holding a knife and—

"You don't understand, Rebecca! You don't under-stand. . . ."

Her hand hovered over the telephone. What if she was wrong? It wouldn't just be Aunt Martha who would be angry with her, then. It would be the whole town! If she called the police and got Mr. Hartwick in trouble—

Oliver!

She could call Oliver! He never told her she didn't understand, or shouldn't worry about something, or treated her like a child. Picking up the telephone, she dialed his number. On the fourth ring she heard his voice. "Oliver? It's Rebecca."

Oliver Metcalf listened carefully as Rebecca told him what she'd seen. As she talked, he recalled Ed Becker's visit to his office that morning, when the lawyer had hinted that Jules Hartwick was behaving strangely. Though Becker hadn't quite come out and said so, it had sounded to Oliver as if Jules was having a breakdown. "Here's what I want you to do," he told Rebecca now. "I want you to call Ed Becker. He's Jules Hartwick's lawyer. Tell him exactly what you've told me, and don't worry about what he might think. Whatever's happened at the Hartwicks', he'll help. All right?"

"But what if I'm wrong, Oliver?" Rebecca fretted. "Aunt Martha always says—"

"Don't worry about what Martha says," Oliver assured her. "If you're wrong, no one but Ed and me will know, and all you're trying to do is help. Just call Ed, and I'll be there as soon as I can." Finding Ed Becker's telephone number on the Rolodex he kept on the kitchen counter, he repeated it twice for Rebecca. He was about to hang up when he heard something in the background. "Rebecca? Do I hear a siren?"

"There's one coming up the street," Rebecca told him. "Just a second." He heard her put the phone down, then, increasingly clear, the wail of a siren. Then he heard Rebecca's voice on the line again.

"It's the police," she said. "A police car just pulled up in front of the Hartwicks'."

"All right," Oliver said. "Call Ed Becker. I'm leaving right now. I'll see you in a little while."

Hanging up the phone, Oliver grabbed his parka from the hook by the door to the garage. He was pulling it on when the phone rang again. This time it was Lois Martin.

"Oliver," she said, "Andrew Sterling and Celeste Hartwick just brought Madeline to the hospitalx. Apparently, Jules tried to kill her. Tried to slash her throat."

"Oh, Jesus," Oliver groaned. "Is she all right?"

"I hope so." Lois sighed. "She's lost a lot of blood and they don't know yet about internal injuries, but they think she has a chance. The nurse called me. I'm going over now to see what else I can find out."

"Good," Oliver told her. "The police just arrived at the Hartwick house. I'm on my way there now. Talk to you later."

Before the phone could ring yet again, he was in his car, turning the ignition key with one hand even as he pressed the remote control for the garage door with the other. He gunned the engine as the door slowly rolled open, sending a cloud of smoke and condensation billowing out of the exhaust pipe. Putting the car into reverse, he backed out, swinging around in the wide arc that would allow him to head straight down the driveway. But in midturn, as the headlights swept across the front of the Asylum, something caught his eye. He slammed on the brakes. The tires instantly lost their traction and the car swerved, leaving the building in darkness. Swearing under his breath, Oliver maneuvered the Volvo back around so that the headlights were once more shining on the building that loomed fifty yards farther up the hill.

Something—*someone*—was on the porch.

For an instant, just an instant, Oliver was confused. But then something in the figure's right hand glinted in the glare of the headlights. Suddenly, he understood.

Jerking the parking brake on but leaving the engine running, Oliver scrambled out of the car and ran up the slope toward the Asylum. He lost his footing in the snow, stumbled, fell to his knees. As he struggled to get up, the figure on the porch raised the knife. "No!" Oliver yelled. "Jules, don't!"

But it was too late. As Oliver watched helplessly, the knife arced downward, its blade plunging deep into Jules Hartwick's belly.

Finally regaining his footing, Oliver charged through the snow. With every step, his feet seemed mired in mud; he hurled himself on, feeling trapped in some terrible nightmare. At last, he came to the porch.

Jules Hartwick, his clothes already soaked with his own blood, was slumped against the Asylum's front door. As Oliver came close to him, his fingers tightened on the haft of the knife, and with a terrible effort he jerked it upward, laying his own belly open. As blood gushed from the gaping wound, he stared up at Oliver. His lips worked spasmodically, and then a sound gurgled from his throat.

"Evil . . ." he whispered. "All around us." His eyes closed and he moaned softly, but then he fixed Oliver with a beseeching stare. "Stop it, Oliver. You have to stop it before it—" He took a gasping, rattling breath. "—before it kills us all. . . ." His body went rigid and his eyes rolled back into his head.

As Jules Hartwick's body relaxed in death, his hands finally lost their grip on the knife. It fell to the porch, clattering eerily in the suddenly silent night.

For a long time Oliver crouched next to his friend. Finally, he stood up and started slowly back to his house. With every step, he heard Jules Hartwick's last words once again.

"You have to stop it . . . before it kills us all."

How, he wondered, was he going to honor Jules's last request when he had no idea what the words meant?

* * *

Midnight. The dark figure moved as silently as a wraith through the blackness of the Asylum, coming at last to the hidden room in which the treasures lay. It was once more the time of the full moon, and the room was suffused with a pale light just strong enough to allow him to admire his collection.

His fingers, sheathed in latex, touched first one object and then another, at last coming to rest on a golden oblong that glittered brightly even in the faint light.

It was an ornate cigarette lighter, cast in the shape of a dragon's head. Ruby red jewels were set in either side as eyes, and the mouth was slightly opened. As the gloved fingers tightened around a trigger in the dragon's neck, a spark flicked deep in its throat. Instantly, a tongue of fire shot from its gaping jaws.

The orange flame danced in the darkness as the shadowed figure pondered.

He already knew for whom the gift was meant; the question now was how to deliver it.

He eased his grip on the dragon's throat.

The flame flickered, then went out.

Soon—very soon—it would flare again.

And when it did, the dragon would strike.

To be continued . . .

The serial thriller continues next month . . .

JOHN SAUL'S THE BLACKSTONE CHRONICLES:
Part Three
Ashes to Ashes:
The Dragon's Flame

Welcome back to Blackstone, the New Hampshire town where evil stalks the night. Death has found a home here, and now the residents must pay. Strange gifts bring mayhem and madness to unsuspecting inhabitants. In Part Three an ornate golden cigarette lighter in the shape of a dragon appears mysteriously somewhere in town. Who will find it? Sweet-natured Rebecca Morrison . . . her straitlaced, embittered Aunt Martha . . . her wild and carefree cousin, Andrea? Will it be attorney Ed Becker . . . or some other unsuspecting soul?

One thing's for sure—the dragon's flame will ignite doom. . . .

To be continued . . .

THE PRESENCE
by John Saul

In all his bone-chilling novels of psychological and supernatural suspense, *New York Times* bestselling author John Saul has proved himself a master of terror. Now prepare yourself for his most frightening novel yet—a story torn from the darkest crevices of night. Something evil has risen around you—but how can you hope to run from a terror you can't even see?

BEWARE
THE PRESENCE!

Coming this summer
A Fawcett Columbine Hardcover Book

JOIN THE CLUB!

Readers of John Saul now can join the John Saul Fan Club by writing to the address below. Members receive an autographed photo of John, newsletters, and advance information about forthcoming publications. Please send your name and address to:

The John Saul Fan Club
P.O. Box 17035
Seattle, Washington 98107

Be sure to visit John Saul at his Web site!
www.johnsaul.com

Visit the town of Blackstone on the Web!
www.randomhouse.com/blackstone
Preview next month's book, talk with other readers, and test your wits against our quizzes to win Blackstone prizes!

TRUE TERROR

ONLY FROM

JOHN SAUL